THE MAN OF BRONZE

Doc Savage was a remarkable man who followed an unusual profession.

Doc was a mental wizard, physical marvel and skilled scientist. His strange profession was the righting of wrongs and punishing of evildoers, particularly in instances when the established authorities seemed unable or unwilling to do the job.

He worked without pay, having a private source of enormous wealth of his own which was rather mysterious.

Bantam Books by Kenneth Robeson
Ask your bookseller for the books you have missed

About Doc Savage
  DOC SAVAGE: HIS APOCALYPTIC LIFE
     by Philip José Farmer

THE ANGRY GHOST

A DOC SAVAGE® ADVENTURE

BY KENNETH ROBESON

BANTAM BOOKS · TORONTO · NEW YORK · LONDON

THE ANGRY GHOST

*A Bantam Book / published by arrangement with
The Condé Nast Publications Inc.*

PRINTING HISTORY
*Originally published February 1940
in* DOC SAVAGE *Magazine*
Bantam edition / January 1977

*Bantam Books are published by Bantam Books, Inc. Its trade-
mark, consisting of the words "Bantam Books" and the por-
trayal of a bantam, is registered in the United States Patent
Office and in other countries. Marca Registrada. Bantam
Books, Inc., 666 Fifth Avenue, New York, New York 10019.*

CONTENTS

Chapter I

THE TROUBLE AT ROCKAWAY

The mystery started at Rockaway Beach. Rockaway is a beach on the south shore of Long Island not far from New York City where white sand stretches into distance beside the endless blue of the Atlantic, and where breakers climb up monotonously and collapse into foam with coughing sounds.

The cautious girl appeared at dawn. She looked around carefully, saw the beach was deserted, and was plainly relieved.

There was one bathhouse open at this ungodly morning hour of five thirty. The Negress attendant shoved out a brown paper envelope.

"Check your valuables in this, miss," the attendant said.

It was one of those envelopes on the flaps of which you write your name for purposes of identification when reclaiming it.

The girl wrote, "*Annabel Lynn.*"

"Oh!" she gasped, and quickly wadded the envelope and dropped it on the sand in front of the bathhouse check-

1

window. "I made a mistake," she explained. "Please give me another envelope."

Her only mistake had been in absent-mindedly writing her correct name on the flap.

She got another envelope and signed it *"Mary Gallagher,"* and filled it with her wrist watch and some money.

While she was doing that, she very carefully stamped the other envelope into the sand with her heel and made sure it was covered with sand.

As soon as Annabel Lynn had entered the bathhouse to change, the Negress attendant, who was a tidy soul, leaned over the counter with the idea of locating the first envelope, the one that had been discarded. She intended to pick it up and put it in the trash basket. The attendant was vaguely surprised when she did not see the envelope. She had not noticed Annabel Lynn carefully burying it.

Annabel Lynn appeared in a bathing suit. She would have done nicely for a magazine cover. Beneath a tight rubber cap, there was visible some soft blond hair. Her lips were nice. Her features were Nordic, beautiful in a regal, classic way. Her figure would have caused an admiring silence, had the beach not been deserted.

The attendant breathed admiringly, "She sho' is a morning glory."

Annabel Lynn walked down to the surf and stood there.

After a while, curiosity impelled the attendant to take another look for the crumpled first envelope. She was puzzled as to what had become of it. So she leaned over the counter again and eyed at the sand.

A small pit now gaped in the sand where Annabel Lynn had buried the wadded envelope.

The attendant stared. That pit hadn't been there a few moments before. Had someone crawled around the corner of the bathhouse and dug—

Something queer happened to Annabel Lynn at this point.

Annabel Lynn suddenly got very rigid, her willowy tall form stiffening and then beginning to tremble. Her trembling was no shiver caused by cold water, but great shuddering that made the girl's hands clench as though someone had spilled ice water on her.

The strangeness of her behavior increased.

Slim hands left her sides and moved with difficulty toward her throat; she clutched at her throat as if trying to throw off something that was strangling her.

Next her fingers raked down over her graceful shoulders —making ripping motions as though trying to pull something loose.

There was nothing visible molesting her. No one on the beach, and only a few early strollers on the boardwalk.

Annabel Lynn suddenly seemed to win her struggle. She staggered backward, as though released. Whirling, she raced along the white sand, long, firm, damp legs flashing in the first rays of morning sunlight.

"Help! Help!" she screamed.

Her voice was full of rending terror.

The soldier was one of the early strollers on the boardwalk. The army gives its men the habit of getting up early, and a number of officers, vacationing at Rockaway, were on the boardwalk. This one wore the regulation officer's uniform of the United States army. He jerked to a halt, and stared.

Annabel Lynn was headed in his direction, so he merely stood and waited.

As the girl drew closer, he understood her terrified cries for help. The army man looked to see who was chasing the tall blond girl, saw nothing, and his jaw sagged.

"What the—"

Because this girl was very pretty, he did the natural thing—he caught the girl, grasping her arm. She was panting.

"What's the trouble, girl?"

"I . . . I—" Annabel Lynn, too breathless to talk, cast a quick glance over her shoulder. The army man noted the girl's pallid cheeks, the tremor that was still upon her lips.

"Something had . . . had hold of me!" she gasped.

Again the soldier gazed up and down the beach—all he saw was gleaming white sand, sky and water.

"Maybe a fish bit you?"

"Eh?"

"Or a lobster pinched you?"

Annabel Lynn shook her blond head quickly. "Hardly!" Her eyes got wider, more horrified. "You couldn't . . . see it. It felt as if something was . . . well it was a stinging sensation all over. As if some kind of an invisible jellyfish had gotten hold of me."

The army officer narrowed his eyes. She was such a lovely girl. He couldn't quite understand her remarks. But she looked sane.

He said, "You're not trying to tell me something grabbed you."

"I . . . yes."

"Now look," said the man soothingly, "let's get this straight—"

"Thank you . . . I . . . I've got to be going," the girl interrupted. She swung on her heel, starting away.

The army man stopped her. "I'm a little worried about you. Sure you're all right?"

"It's quite all right now. I . . . I must hurry. I have a car parked back there a ways. Thank you."

But the army man was persistent—this girl was pretty enough to make any man persistent. "Wait! Maybe I can catch that dingus that had hold of you."

"Don't be silly," she said quickly.

"But—"

"You see, it's . . . gone," the girl explained. "It's gone. And even if it wasn't, you wouldn't be able to see it."

"It's—" The officer's sharp eyes popped. "*What* is gone? What the heck is this, anyway?"

"Please—please forget it!" the girl said. She walked rapidly toward the roadway, slim legs driving her feet through the loose, slippery sand.

Two men had been watching the incident. The pair were so concealed that the girl would not have seen their figures even had she been seeking them. The beach sand had formed small dunes. Protruding from the tops of the dunes were bunches of sea grass, tall and scraggly grass that concealed the two men as they lay flat. They did not have nice faces. They hardly looked like the kind who would spend time enjoying the view at the seashore.

One growled, "See that! She was tellin' that army guy something!"

"That wasn't so good," his partner agreed. He fingered something—the check-room envelope on which Annabel Lynn had signed her correct name by mistake. "Good thing I crawled around the boathouse and got this envelope. I figured there was something familiar about her."

"Yeah—she wasn't on that beach to go swimmin'."

"Sure. You saw how she acted."

"Yes. She got touched by it. She was right in the way! And she's got some idea where it was, I bet."

The other man's hard-looking eyes widened, and he said with some awe, "Jeepers! You think she told that army guy what it *was?*"

"She might've."

"Hell!"

"I'll say it's hell. In that case, we'll have to take care of *both* of them!"

"Match you to see who takes the girl."

They matched nickels.

"I get the dame!" the heavier of the two chuckled.

The pair separated, one trailing the army officer, to whom Annabel Lynn had spoken.

The other, crouching low and keeping behind the dunes, followed the tall blond girl as she secured her clothing, and without changing, hurried to her car. The machine was a small green coupé, parked at the end of a road that ended here at the dunes. It would be necessary, the pursuer saw, for the girl to back the car and turn to leave.

Just as the girl reached the coupé door, the man got up and ran. He was not worried about being seen now. The girl still had to turn the car. There was plenty of time to overtake her.

The man made one error. He did not figure on a woman being able to drive backward almost as expertly as forward. The girl got a glimpse of the man. She leaped into the car. A motor kept warm by the morning sun snapped quickly into life. She slapped the car in gear, gunned the motor, handled the machine deftly. The man came leaping after the car.

But the girl got away.

The man stood staring, and sweat came out on his face, and his eyes suddenly were full of fear. He muttered, "Now this is going to be a nice mess!"

Annabel Lynn drove at high speed until she reached an arterial highway, then drove more carefully. Only once did she stop, and then to take only a moment to slip her dress over her head. She still wore beach slippers.

She stopped at all red lights, observed all the speed limits, carefully doing nothing that might attract the attention of a police officer.

Yet she looked frightened enough to call a dozen policemen. Her cheeks had lost color. Her wide gray-blue eyes held the stare of a person who had experienced shock.

From time to time, as the girl drove, she raised a slender hand to her throat and touched her arms or her shoulders. Each time she made this motion, she shuddered.

At a midtown Manhattan hotel, a doorman took charge of the car and Annabel Lynn hurried through the lobby, got her key and went to an elevator. On the eleventh floor, she waited in the carpeted hallway until the elevator door slid shut and the cage departed. She looked furtively up and down the long hall. Seeing no one, she stepped quickly to a door. Her hands were trembling.

When she had locked the door behind her, she collapsed on the bed. Her whole form shook with uncontrollable shuddering.

After calmness came back, she sat up, and her mouth was determined.

She went to the table where she had dropped her purse.

The object she removed from the purse was a small black notebook that seemed to be filled with names and numbers. Annabel Lynn thumbed the pages of the booklet, then her lips moved silently as she memorized a number. She sat down at the phone near the head of the bed, gave the number to the hotel operator, waited several moments while the connection was being made.

Her decision to call the phone number apparently had lifted weight from her shoulders—she was obviously relieved.

A supervisor's voice said, "Pardon me, but are you calling the unlisted phone number of Clark Savage, Jr.?"

"That is correct. I must speak to Doc Savage!"

"Sorry," said the supervisor, "but that number does not answer."

Slowly, almost dazedly, Annabel Lynn hung up—gone was the relieved expression of a moment ago; her eyes widened uneasily.

Chapter II

MESSAGE FOR DOC

Annabel Lynn had tried to contact Doc Savage at ten thirty that morning, at noon, at two o'clock, then at four. She did not leave her room and at six she decided to risk the chance—she was obviously afraid to leave her hotel room—and go see the bronze man in person.

She donned black—black dress, hose, shoes and hat, even wore a black veil that concealed her features. Black was a color that permitted one to merge well with the night.

When finally, she was ready, she opened her room door cautiously, peered up and down the hallway, then moved quickly toward the elevators. Later she was in a cab headed downtown, without having been molested.

She changed cabs three times, and made absolutely certain that she was not being trailed.

Then she directed the cab to one of New York City's tallest buildings. An elevator whisked her swiftly to the topmost floor, the quick ascent setting her ears to ringing.

There was a long, plain hallway of rich marble.

There was also a man.

The man was about forty, well-dressed, slim-waisted; he carried a black cane. He was not bad-looking.

A legend on a bronze-colored door read, *"Clark Savage, Jr."*

The tall man stepped aside as Annabel Lynn moved to the door, pressed a buzzer and waited. The well-dressed man paused and stared at her in a well-bred way.

"You looking for Doc Savage?" he asked.

"I—" the girl hesitated.

"Doc is out of town," the stranger advised her. "I'm afraid you'll find no one else there, either."

Behind the black-net veil which partially concealed her features, Annabel Lynn's eyes were distraught.

Doc Savage was a remarkable man who followed an unusual profession. Doc was a mental wizard, physical marvel and skilled scientist. His strange profession was the righting of wrongs and punishing of evil-doers, particularly in such instances when the established authorities seemed unable or unwilling to do the job. He worked without pay, having a private source of enormous wealth of his own which was rather mysterious.

The elaborately dressed man said, "Perhaps I can help you. I am Brigadier General Theodore Marley Brooks, one of the assistants of Doc Savage—"

"Ham Brooks!" Annabel Lynn gasped.

"Yes."

"If I can't find Doc Savage, maybe I should talk to you."

The man smiled. "Maybe we could have dinner together while you talk."

"I . . . well, yes," the girl said, realizing she was hungry.

The man moved to the elevator, pressed the button and soon they were descending.

"I have a car waiting," the man continued, smiling pleasantly.

A quick shower had come up, and the streets were wet. A large closed car stood at the curb near the building entrance.

"My friends," the dapper man said.

Men were seated in the back of the car. The driver leaned over, opened the door on the curb side, and the girl's companion said, "We will squeeze in the front. Unconventional, but if you don't mind. I will drop my friends at their club."

Annabel Lynn climbed in, sat between driver and the dapper man. The car pulled away from the curb. Her gaze moved to the rear-view mirror—faces in the rear were a trifle vague in the dusk of early evening. Then she gave a start. There was something wrong with the whole situation.

She gasped, "One of those men in the back—he was on Rockaway Beach this morning!"

From the rear seat, there was a satisfied, harsh laugh. "Sis, you should have remembered that sooner!"

The heavy car began doing forty on the wet pavement. The driver swung, took a side street, and thereafter kept away from thoroughfares that were too thickly congested. The girl sat stiffly. Warning words came from the well-dressed man seated so close to her.

"You shouldn't have tried to phone Doc Savage," he said, and laughed silkily. "Or to see him, either."

Annabel Lynn was puzzled. "But how—"

"Twenty bucks looked good to that switchboard operator at your hotel, sister! She told us. She kept you from getting through to the bronze guy."

Behind the veil, Annabel Lynn's eyes grew wide.

One of the men continued, "That army guy you talked to on the beach this mornin' got away, babe. So now we want to know just what you told him. Also, *why did you want to reach Doc Savage?*"

Annabel Lynn compressed her lips, said nothing.

"You know what was happening there on the beach this morning, don't you?" the man growled.

The girl kept silent.

Ahead, a busy intersection loomed. The car driver was timing his speed so he would hit the green light. In the middle of the intersection stood a traffic cop. The driver removed his foot from the gas peddle; he was taking no chances on arousing the suspicions of the traffic cop.

Suddenly, Annabel Lynn's foot shot out, came down on the brake. Down as hard as she could push.

Rubber squealed as the wheels locked. Tires failed to hold on the wet pavement. The heavy car went into a skid, slithered sidewise, smacked into a car in the adjoining traffic lane. A car behind crashed into them. There was uproar. The cop was running toward them.

The policeman yelled, "Hey, what d'you think this is?"

Annabel Lynn scrambled out of the car, ducked for the sidewalk with flashing speed.

The cop yelled, "Hey!"

But Annabel Lynn's slender tall figure moved like a shadow between stalled machines. She made a zigzag course through a triple line of stalled cars, reached the other side of the street where traffic was still moving in the opposite direction. An empty cab was just rolling past, and the girl hailed the driver and climbed into the cab's rear seat.

She ordered, "Pennsylvania Station. Hurry!"

As they rolled down a ramp beneath the great railroad station, Annabel Lynn took a check book from her purse and made out a check to the hotel at which she'd been stopping. She handed the check to the cab driver after she got out.

"Please take that to the hotel. It will pay my bill. Ask the baggage clerk to have my bags forwarded to the Union Station in Washington, D. C." The girl handed over a five-dollar bill along with the check. "And this is for yourself."

The driver beamed around a missing tooth. "You bet, ma'am. And thanks! You know they ain't many people trust a cab driver like this. I appreciate it."

Even this precaution of not returning to her hotel worried her—perhaps the men who sought her would learn of the forwarding of her baggage. That was why she had given no hotel address in Washington—had used only the Union Station. It would be safer.

She learned that she had a half hour to wait for the next Washington train. She bought her ticket, an evening paper, then located a deserted corner in the huge waiting room and sat down on a bench that faced away from the vast rotunda.

An item on the first page of the paper got her attention.

HOT WORDS FLY
IN ARMY CEMENT CASE

Repeated angry exchanges of words today marked the progress of the army's examination into the strange matter of how the gun foundations at Fort Atlantic came to collapse.

Henry T. Neely, contractor who built the foundations, at one time leaped up and screamed "Liar!" at army officers.

The girl read the article with a pale-faced, unnatural interest.

It seemed the United States government had let out a contract for construction of new antiaircraft gun emplacements at Fort Atlantic, and months had been spent placing reinforcements and pouring cement for gun bases that, it was said, were second to none in the country.

A few days before, a government engineer had made a routine inspection—when he finished, a lot of people were wild-eyed; none of them more wild-eyed than the contractor.

For during the inspection, the startling fact had developed that the extensive gun foundations were *worthless.* Sand and cement and gravel and even steel had disintegrated, fallen apart.

Government engineers blamed the trouble on too little cement, too much sand. The contractor—Henry T. Neely was one of the biggest in business—had called the government men liars. He offered bills and figures to prove that he had used the correct proportion of sand, cement and gravel.

But the army engineers were adamant. Seeing was believing, in their opinion. Any damn fool could now see that the new foundations were worthless.

The girl rubbed a trembling hand across her eyes, as though trying to blot out the whole thing. Then, on a sudden impulse, she glanced up at a wall clock. There was still twenty minutes until her train time.

There was another item, this one short, which interested the girl. It read:

NOTED LAWYER URGES SOCIAL
REFORM IN WASHINGTON TO
PRESS LEGISLATION

Brigadier General Theodore Marley "Ham" Brooks, noted lawyer, is in Washington to urge congress to adopt a program of free public-hospital care. With him is Lieutenant Colonel Andrew Blodgett "Monk" Mayfair, the famous industrial chemist.

Both Ham Brooks and Monk Mayfair are associated with the mysterious international figure, Doc Savage, sometimes known as the Man of Bronze.

Annabel Lynn went to a nearby newsstand, obtained two dollars' worth of change, hurried to a phone booth. She put through a call to Washington, D. C.

Finally, a sharp voice said at the other end of the wire, "Hello?"

Annabel Lynn gave a quick gasp of relief. She said, "Warren?"

The voice lost its sharpness and became gentle and anxious. "Annabel! You're all right? I've been worried about you, my dear!"

"Yes . . . yes, I'm all right. I'll be in Washington sometime before morning. But first, there is something you must do for me—you've heard of Doc Savage?"

There was a short pause. Then the man's voice replied, "Well, quite! I'll say. The fellow is some sort of scientific genius, judging from what I've heard."

"I've been trying to reach him."

"But—"

"And he apparently is not in New York. But two men who are his associates are in Washington now. You must arrange a meeting with them for me."

The voice at the other end of the wire protested, "But that has nothing to do with—"

"Warren," the girl said insistently. "You've *got* to do that. It's . . . important."

"All right, then," the man answered. "I imagine they will attend the big dinner tomorrow night at the Embassy Club. Everyone who is anybody will be there."

Annabel Lynn hung up. Later, on the express which rolled slowly out of the station tunnel, she reflected that Warren would get her the meeting she had requested. Warren was efficient.

Chapter III

TRAILED

Brigadier General Theodore Marley Brooks, known as Ham to his friends and those who could outrun him, did not like the nickname. He was one of the nation's leading lawyers, a Harvard graduate, also one of the aids of Doc Savage.

The apish man was his partner, Andrew Blodgett Mayfair. For obvious reasons, he was nicknamed Monk. Though his appearance and actions gave no indication, Monk had brains. He was a renowned chemist.

"I hope that girl," Ham said angrily, "is pretty enough to make up for some of these troubles."

"What girl?" Monk asked. Girls invariably interested Monk.

"A fellow named Warren—I met him somewhere—telephoned me this afternoon," Ham explained, "and said she wanted very much to meet us at the Embassy Club tonight."

The Embassy Club occupied one of those regal old buildings off Pennsylvania Avenue. Twenty years ago, the place had been one of the richest embassies of a European ruler since deposed, and the all but gold-plated interior had been transformed into as richly exclusive a spot, probably, as the nation boasted. There was refinement in the surroundings, elegance; there was one of the best orchestras—no slam-bang bunch of wild Indians called a swing band, but a soft ensemble that played with feeling.

Inside, no man was dressed in anything as vulgar as a tux. Full tails was the thing. Preferably a ribbon across the chest, also.

"I'm jolly well glad to meet you again," said a young man who was rather more slim and handsome than Monk liked them.

"This is Warren—Warren Allen," Ham told the homely chemist.

Monk put Warren Allen down in his mental black book as a rather elegant piece of manhood. Not that one should hold appearances against a fellow—particularly when the appearances were much on the handsome side. Monk really had nothing against Warren Allen except the fellow's good looks. That, and the fellow's English accent, which was a little on the heavy edge.

"Pleased t'meetcha," Monk said unenthusiastically.

"Right over here," advised Warren Allen, "is the young lady who wishes to meet you."

He led them over to the vision that was Annabel Lynn, and performed introductions.

Then, to Monk's pleased astonishment, Warren Allen had the good grace to excuse himself and walk away.

"This," Monk said instantly, "is going to be a wonderful evening. Meeting a girl as pretty as you starts it off with a crash like thunder."

"I want to talk to you," the girl said.

They found a small private anteroom. Annabel Lynn said, "I . . . I tried to reach Doc Savage, and he wasn't there." She looked around, as though fearful even someone might be listening.

"Yes?" Ham suggested.

"It's . . . I'm afraid. It's not even safe to talk here. Could you meet me some place else, say in an hour?"

There was fear in the depths of the girl's eyes, and she

asked, "You'll meet me? You see, *I've got something to tell Doc Savage!*"

Ham nodded.

"Meet me at the La Grecia restaurant at Norfolk and Y streets," the girl suggested.

"In half an hour," Ham agreed.

After the girl had departed, Monk put on a remarkable villainous green topcoat which he wore over his full dress suit, and they hailed a cab.

Ham rested his polished black cane—a sword-cane—which he always carried, against the seat beside him. "That girl is scared."

"Yeah. There must be something wrong. Maybe we oughta contact Doc. We're only down here on business, to lobby for free hospital care for everybody. There was nothin' said about gettin' into trouble."

Ham glanced over his shoulder once or twice. Their cab turned various corners. Ham continued to watch over his shoulder.

"Well, if you ask me, trouble is at hand."

"Eh?"

"We're being followed."

Monk looked suddenly interested. "Where?"

"It's that sedan. Been trailing us for the last few minutes."

The trailing sedan was not in sight when they finally pulled up before the small curtained-window restaurant that had been mentioned as the meeting place. And neither was blond Annabel Lynn in view.

To their astonishment, Warren Allen came running out of the eating place just as they climbed out of the cab. In fact, Warren Allen rushed out so fast that he crashed into Monk. He started to make apologies, then took a look at the hairy chemist's green topcoat—which hardly befitted the "soup and tails" Monk was wearing—and shuddered.

"My word!" Warren Allen exploded. "These Americans! There's positively no telling what rags they'll wear next."

Monk was tempted to let go with a haymaker. Ham kicked and took bark from Monk's shins.

"Nice little restaurant," Ham said. "I see you like it, too."

Warren Allen gave Ham a direct look from level gray

eyes. "My word, quite! Yes. But . . . oh . . . to tell the truth I was sent here by Miss Annabel Lynn to meet you."

Monk said, "Where's the girl?"

Warren Allen looked worried. "I . . . well, she's at another spot."

"Where?" Monk was getting suspicious.

"The Treasury Building."

"The Treasury—what the heck! This time of night? That place would be closed now."

The tall blond man, who was so obviously English, agreed. "Quite!" he said. "But she went there and she asked me to bring you."

"Why?"

"I do not know."

Warren Allen had a debonair manner that was not even second to smartly dressed Ham's. The two men, Ham and Warren Allen, sized one another up, and each apparently admired the other's choice in wearing apparel. Monk was disgusted.

"Let's go!" the homely chemist growled.

Warren Allen said, "I have my own car parked just ahead there."

He indicated a sleek-looking, expensive roadster. Then he mentioned two direct routes to the Treasury Building, and told Ham which one to take.

Monk and Ham got back in their own cab.

Warren Allen called, "Watch for a green cab when you get there. She is in such a cab and may be waiting in the machine."

Warren Allen left in one direction; Ham and hairy Monk took another. Both routes would bring them to the great stone Treasury Building located near the White House. On the rear seat of the cab, dapper Ham fooled with his black cane.

"Funny," he remarked. "We no sooner met Annabel Lynn than something went wrong. She was scared, wanted to see us in privacy. She didn't show up. Also, there was that large sedan which was following us."

Monk said abruptly, "Did you say *was* followin' us?"

"Of course."

"Look!" Monk said.

The large sedan had suddenly reappeared, and had

swerved across the narrow street in front of them, block-ing their path.

As the cab driver slammed on his brakes to avoid a crash, grim-faced Monk flung open the cab door and went piling out into the street.

Chapter IV

CARS IN THE NIGHT

It was late in the night and there was no traffic on this particular narrow thoroughfare; the long sedan had blocked the path of the cab completely.

Men now piled out of the blockading sedan. A street lamp nearby cast feeble glow over faces that were coarse and grim. There were at least a half-dozen assailants.

One snarled, "That's the pair! Grab 'em!"

But Monk already had made up his mind about who was to do the grabbing. He dived for the group. His great fists started pumping.

Three men piled on Monk, dumped him to the street. Another started jumping up and down on him. Monk grabbed assorted legs, twisted, howled.

The cab driver headed for points distant.

Ham never used Monk's roughhouse tactics. He unsheathed his sword-cane. It flashed in the faint glow of street lights.

Ham began pricking men with the blade. His victims soon got down on knees, as though looking for a hole in

18

which to hide, then one by one sprawled out and lay still. For the tip of Ham's cane contained a violent anaesthetic drug which produced brief unconsciousness.

Monk was still swinging. Practically at empty air. Then he realized there was only a single figure facing him, and he almost swung at it before he decided it was Ham.

"I was just gettin' warmed up!" Monk yelled. "Why'd you use that sword-cane and spoil—"

Blam! The one who looked like Ham hauled off and let Monk have a right to the jaw.

Monk went down in a pink haze. For several moments, the hairy chemist's brain did spins. Then he realized vaguely that someone was helping him to his feet.

It was Ham doing the helping.

Monk bellowed, "You hit me, shyster!" and cut loose with a steaming right. Ham stepped nimbly aside. "Listen, stupid!" Ham snapped. "Take a look at that fellow there on the ground!"

Monk looked.

The supine individual closely resembled smartly dressed Ham. He wore well-tailored clothes; in the poor light, Monk had mistaken the fellow for Ham.

Monk said, "Blazes!" He rubbed a numb jaw. "Where's that Treasury Building where that danged Englishman said the girl would be waiting?"

Ham pointed with his sword-cane. "Two blocks down the street yonder."

The stone building was a great grim stone tube in the night. Windows were dark.

Abruptly, a cab rolled under the nearby street light, stopped—then started away swiftly after the occupant had opened the door and leaned out to stare.

Monk yelled, "Looks like our girl in that hack!"

Ham barked, "And the cab is green!" He was remembering Warren Allen's statement that the girl would be in a green cab.

"This is a frame-up!" Monk howled. "The girl and that Allen led us into a trap."

Monk said, "I'll get her! You watch these mugs!"

Monk started running, trying to overtake the girl's cab. Annabel Lynn apparently held the key to whatever this mystery was all about.

And then the shaking sensation seized Monk and Ham.

Monk stopped, astounded by the ripping, tearing-apart sensation that went through his whole body. It felt as though unseen, giant hands—hundreds of hands—had grasped them and were shaking them.

They gagged, staggered around, clutched at various parts of their own bodies.

Ham gasped, "Ugg . . . I . . . ah . . . Jehoshaphat!"

The peculiar sensation stopped. As swiftly as it had come, it was gone. Monk let out a long howl.

"What could that have been?" Monk gasped.

Ham looked all around, saw nothing.

"You guess," he said.

Then he saw that Monk was suddenly staring at the huge Treasury Building. Monk shouted, "*Look!*"

A part of the great Treasury Building had started to collapse. A single corner of the massive edifice was giving way in a miniature land slide of pulverized rock, cement and sand, the stuff pouring out over the sidewalk, over-flowing into the street. Fixtures and equipment that were obviously a part of a room somewhere in that part of the building, followed out into the street. The land slide of rock and sand made a great racket. People seemingly ap-pearing from nowhere, there began to be bedlam. Front doors of the Treasury Building burst open; excited guards piled out into the street. There was the moan of police-car sirens; soon blue-coated men were swarming all around the place. Cars were jammed in the wide streets, more machines rolling up and adding to the confusion.

Monk said, "Blazes! A hold-up, I'll bet."

"You didn't see any gunmen trying to get away from there, did you?"

Monk had to admit he had seen no one trying to escape from the place.

"And you didn't hear any explosion, did you?" Ham added.

"Then what was it?"

"Search me. It was as though the corner just caved out of that building."

"Yeah," Monk murmured.

Both of them had forgotten their late foes. Then they remembered, and went back.

Their attackers were all gone. They must have been helped to escape.

The time was approximately twelve twenty.

Monk said thoughtfully. "Damn queer that girl left word she was coming here—and then those mugs tried to get us. It still looks like a trick to me."

The only vehicle nearby was a large milk truck moving slowly along the street a little ahead of Monk and Ham. It was the type of milk truck used to supply hotels and restaurants.

"Hey, truck!" Monk called. "How's a chance for a lift?"

The driver turned his head slightly, said over his shoulder to someone in the vanlike body, "Hear that, Ambrose? These lugs want a lift. They didn't know we was plannin' to invite 'em!"

The man got out of the truck, and Monk and Ham found themselves staring into the muzzle of a gun that loomed big in the murk.

From behind the gun, a voice ordered, "Climb in, pals. It's our night to be lucky."

The leader of their new acquaintances seemed to be named Ambrose. Ambrose had a lot of face, a lot of jaw, and a lot of gun. He waggled the gun, covering Monk and Ham as they swung into the rear of the truck.

There was a partition across half of the rear truck compartment.

They never did see what was in the other half of the truck, although it didn't strike them as important at the time.

In dressing for the affair at the Embassy Club, Monk and Ham had left behind their weapons, including the machine pistols which Doc Savage's men usually carried. Getting Monk into full dress had been hard enough, and there would have been no space left to conceal a shoulder holster anyway.

"Nice going, Ambrose," a voice said.

Ambrose, it appeared, was backed up by at least two hard-looking henchmen, the second of whom added, "Lie down, you two!"

Monk was the kind of fellow who needed a lot of convincing. His bull-like head lowered, and he dived at the nearest man. His fists started pumping. Ham, who still carried his sword-cane, tried to swing it into use. But the surprise attack failed. Someone dropped a gun butt—it felt like the Washington Monument—on the hairy chemist's head and he lost all interest in the battle. A fist was used on Ham's jaw.

Later, when they woke up, there was no longer swaying motion of the truck moving. Everything was oddly silent. It was also incredibly dark.

Monk, always a humorist of sorts, muttered, "I ain't dead, I hope."

Ham's voice said, "Shut up, you misfit. I'm trying to figure out where we are."

The lawyer's words came out of the blackness somewhere close to Monk. The chemist tried to rise, realized that he was tied up hand and foot. He asked, "Where the blazes are we?"

"Garage of some kind, I think," Ham said. "They just went out to another room. Some of them are going to try to catch the girl."

"You mean *the* girl?" Monk asked in the darkness. He was trying to squirm around to reach his feet, but his hands were tied behind him.

"Yes—Annabel Lynn," Ham said. "Seems they're looking for her, too. And from what I overheard, I think they know where to find her. Damn these ropes!"

Monk said, "Wait." He inched across the cement floor and located Ham, got close to him, instructed, "Use your teeth. My vest pocket. There's a cigar in there."

"Cigar?" the lawyer asked. "What good will—"

"Get the blasted thing out!"

Ham twisted his neck until he was able to grip the cigar with his teeth, pull it out and drop it to the floor. Monk rolled over, found the thing with his bound hands, broke it and felt powder run on to the floor.

Monk explained, "Some stuff Doc invented. It'll rot these cords as soon as it's been exposed to the air a second."

Monk was pressing his wrists down close to the cement, against the powder. He tugged. A strand parted. Another. The bindings fell apart. Monk untied his ankles and got Ham free.

"Nice goin' on my part, eh?" Monk chuckled.

"Unless you want your head shot off by these guys, keep quiet! They're somewhere outside in another room."

They crawled through the darkness, hands outstretched

to intercept any object in their path. They reached a wall. There was a door. Ham slowly eased it open.

The door gave onto a weed-filled field that was bare and desolate in a starry night. Thick silence was everywhere.

Monk piped sadly, "An' I was gonna muss up them guys!" He looked around. "Blazes, this isn't a garage. It's just a shack in an old dump."

It was true. There was no sign of truck, men or habitation. Far off in the distance, there was a reddish glow in the sky.

Ham pointed at the glow. "Probably Washington," he said.

"Danged if it ain't a long way off. I hope we don't have to walk."

Ham, his usually meticulous person somewhat battered and decrepit, started toward a dusty road that was nearby. He said, "You can wait and see if you can sprout wings, if you want to."

Monk scowled and followed. His evening clothes were torn. His starched shirt was ripped open over his hairy chest. There was a lump on his forehead.

He said to Ham, "Can you figure it out, smart-pants."

"Those men who jumped us knew we were going to meet her. They were working with the gang on that phony milk truck near the Treasury Building. They didn't want us to talk to that girl."

"Why?"

"I don't know."

"I thought you were going to figure out all the answers."

Ham lapsed into an offended silence.

Later, "I wonder what was in the other half of that truck?" he pondered aloud.

Monk apparently didn't hear that.

"Where we gonna find the girl?" the homely chemist grunted.

"The logical place to start would be her hotel."

"What one?"

"How would I know? We'll just have to try 'em all."

"Maybe she don't live in a hotel. We don't know anything about her."

"Oh, stop trying to think of things to make it worse than it is."

"Maybe we ought to tell Doc about the whole business." For once, Ham agreed. "Perhaps we ought."

That started both of them thinking about getting a phone call through to Doc Savage, in New York. They quickened their pace through the quiet night, and did not see a car, moving without lights, far back in the road behind them.

Monk stopped suddenly.

"Hey—blazes!" he exploded.

A remarkable-looking figure had come out of the darkness with a flashlight and a gun. They made out the gun— it was pointed at them—as soon as their eyes became accustomed to the flashlight glare.

"My name," said the weird-looking one, "is Nanny Hanks. We had better get acquainted."

Chapter V

MYSTERY AT 12:20

In New York City, Doc Savage drove into the unusual basement garage of his skyscraper headquarters. He had just arrived from a waterfront hangar, where he had left Long Tom Roberts and Renny Renwick, two of his group of five associates. For some days, Doc and the two men had been working on a diving-bell device that the bronze man was hoping to perfect at his Hudson River warehouse-hangar. Long Tom and Renny were cleaning up details and would join him shortly.

Standing beside his car, Doc Savage was of unusual size; he could easily glance across the roof of the big machine. His shoulders did not seem unnaturally broad until one compared their width to the car-door opening. The whole remarkable physique of the bronze giant was of the same symmetrical largeness. His skin was unusual, as though bronzed by tropical suns; his hair, which lay smooth against his head, was of a bronze hue somewhat darker.

His eyes were most remarkable. They were like flake-gold, stirred continually with a restlessness that gave some indication of the activity of the bronze man's mind.

Doc Savage showed no outward sign that he knew a man was trailing him.

The stranger had jumped the car as it slipped into the driveway leading to the private garage in the skyscraper basement.

Now the man suddenly came out from behind the car with a big gun in his fist and a snarl on his lips.

"I've heard plenty about you!" the man growled. "And I'm one boy who don't take chances."

He fired point-blank at the bronze man's chest. Doc Savage fell to the cement floor.

The gunman—he was well over six feet tall—came forward and poked a big foot at the bronze man's limp figure. He laughed harshly.

"I wasn't any fool," he said.

Turning quickly, the gunman moved to a switch panel located on one wall of the basement garage. When Doc Savage had driven into the place, doors had opened automatically at the approach of the big limousine, but they had closed again as soon as the bronze man had driven the car inside.

The doors were obviously controlled by an electric radio device; they were also armor-plated. The doors would be opened mechanically from the switch panel, and it was thus the gunman opened them now.

Two more thugs slipped quickly into the garage. They grinned when they saw the bronze man lying on the cement floor.

One said, "Ambrose said we better finish this bronze guy off right now. It sure as hell worked!"

"You think the girl reached him?"

"Annabel Lynn?—that's what Ambrose was worried about. What's the difference now? He's dead."

"Maybe we better search him to make sure he ain't carryin' any evidence she might have given him—in case she did see him."

The man with the gun bent down, laid his weapon on the floor, started to go through the bronze man's inside coat pocket. Several blurred things happened.

Doc Savage came up off the floor with smooth motion. The tall gunman was slammed through the air, struck the wall, let out a grunt, folded in a heap. The other two men let out yells, reached for shoulder holsters, dived toward the bronze man. But Doc moved with incredible speed. He seized the nearest man, hurled him into his partner. Both tangled on the floor.

The bronze man's hand went to a special vest that he wore beneath his coat; with his fingers he flung a small glass capsule to the hard floor. It broke. Liquid came from the thing, vaporized, turning into gas.

Slowly, the men went limp. Arms and legs spread out slackly as they became unconscious.

Doc Savage continued to hold his breath for another half minute. While he did so, he moved toward a wall switch, flicked it, and an exhaust fan made a humming sound in the basement garage. The gas, which smelled and had a faint color, was soon drawn from the garage. While this was going on, the bronze man stood outside. The gas capsule, one which he had perfected himself, had contained a harmless anæsthetic drug that produced temporary unconsciousness.

Doc examined the would-be killers. The bronze man had never seen the assailants before. He had no idea of the reason for the attack on his life. But apparently it had something to do with the girl—a girl named Annabel Lynn, who had been trying to see him.

The garage doors opened—controlled by a radio device which the bronze man's aids had installed in their car— and Renny and Long Tom drove into the garage. Both men—associates of Doc Savage—stared at the men on the floor.

"Holy cow!" Renny boomed.

Renny was a giant in stature, with hands like quart pails, a long, puritanical face wreathed with undertaker gloom.

Doc Savage briefly explained what had occurred.

"Too bad we weren't here," muttered Long Tom.

Long Tom asked, "What's behind this?"

"Apparently it has something to do with a girl."

"Girl?"

Doc nodded. "It has me puzzled. We might try truth serum."

The "truth serum" was a variation of the type used sometimes by police laboratories, and was one of the bronze man's own formulas.

"How come the bullet didn't kill you?" Long Tom asked.

"Bullet-proof vest," Doc explained.

Before the assailants regained their senses, they were bound and taken to the skyscraper headquarters of the bronze man, and in the great book-lined library on the eighty-sixth floor ærie Doc Savage administered truth serum to the trio, using a hypo needle. The gas effects wore off, leaving them under the influence of the truth serum—in a state somewhat resembling drunkenness.

Renny and Long Tom propped the man in a chair, and he answered—he was powerless to do otherwise—such questions as they put, although his speech was incoherent, frequently not at all understandable.

"Her name is Annabel Lynn," they decided he said in answers to questions as to who the girl was.

"Why is she trying to reach me?"

"Because she was out on Rockaway Beach when something happened, and Ambrose figures she knows too much."

"Too much about what?"

"I don't know. Ambrose wouldn't tell us."

Renny boomed, "Holy cow! Who is Ambrose?"

"The guy who hired us," the man mumbled stupidly, after several attempts.

"Where is he?"

"Washington, D. C."

Further questioning only made it more apparent that these three crooks worked for the someone named Ambrose. As to who Ambrose was or what kind of scheme he was perpetrating, the men had no idea.

It was only evident that Ambrose was immensely worried over something the girl, Annabel Lynn, had shown she knew at Rockaway Beach.

Both Renny and Long Tom tried further questioning of the captives, but learned nothing additional to help clear up the reason for the attempt on Doc's life.

Doc said, "They have told us all they know. They're ready for the college."

Renny got on a telephone and made arrangements for the transfer of the three would-be killers to the "college" —a strange institution in upstate New York where criminals, through delicate brain operations instituted by Doc, had all remembrance of their past wiped out. After being trained, these crooks who had "forgotten" their pasts were released, cured of all criminal tendencies, thenceforth to lead the lives of normal, worth-while citizens.

Doc entered the big laboratory—his headquarters consisted of library, lab and reception room occupying one whole floor of the great skyscraper—a sanctum where he could work undisturbed. The bronze man often worked through the night here, perfecting some new device or formula for the benefit of mankind.

A strange thing happened when Doc entered the lab. He stopped.

Practically every delicate instrument in one corner of the laboratory had been smashed.

It was not as though someone had entered the bronze man's laboratory and smashed the valuable instruments with an ax. It was simply as though delicate apparatus had fallen apart, disintegrated, crumpled in their sensitive racks and mountings. One set of instruments in particular drew the bronze giant's gaze. Protected by glass panels, the devices stood on a large, insulated cabinet. But now the glass was shattered; instruments that had cost thousands of dollars lay broken within.

Mounted on one carefully constructed base was a seismoscope, a device for recording the disturbances of earthquake nature.

Located at some distance was a graph attachment which dictated the exact time of any earth disturbance. For example, a blast during the construction work in the new Sixth Avenue subway, in New York, would have been recorded by the sensitive machine, and the exact time shown.

The graph showed that the machine had collapsed to bits at exactly 12:20 p. m.

It was a confounding piece of mystery. There was no indication that anyone had entered the laboratory—the burglar alarms on the doors and windows were highly sensitive and would have shown the visit of any prowler —and there seemed no plausible explanation for the shattered condition of the instruments.

In several spots, plaster had fallen off the walls, and even masonry was cracked and crumbling. At one point the bronze man noted that a steel supporting beam was exposed. He kicked it. The beam crumpled for a short distance, the fragments of steel rattling over the floor like ball bearings.

Chapter VI

NANNY HANKS

It was shortly later that Doc Savage received a telephone call from Ham and Monk, in Washington. Ham spoke from a cigar-store booth in the suburbs of the capital. The lawyer told about meeting Annabel Lynn, of the run-in with the fake milk-truck thugs. Doc listened attentively. "Why does Annabel Lynn wish to see me?"

Ham's voice was disgusted over the wire. "Search me, Doc! And now she's disappeared. Right after that Treasury Building trouble, we saw her leaving in a hurry—"

"Treasury Building?"

"Part of the Treasury Building collapsed!" Ham explained. "It just seemed to disintegrate. Queerest thing you ever saw."

Doc Savage's flake-gold eyes became restless.

"Collapsed?"

"That's right. Just a little after midnight. Guess the newspapers haven't got it out yet."

"What was the *exact* time?" Doc Savage asked.

For a moment, there was silence. Then the lawyer said,

"Well, I happened to glance at my watch, Doc. It was just twenty minutes after twelve."

"And there was no explosion?"

"No."

The bronze man reached a decision. "We will leave for Washington immediately. It is imperative that we locate the girl. At what hotel are you stopping?"

Ham named the hotel.

"We should be there in two hours," Doc advised. "The trip from here should take no longer than that."

Doc Savage turned to Renny and Long Tom.

"Renny," Doc said quietly, "you are acquainted with Major Woods at Fort Atlantic, on Long Island?"

"Yes."

"You are interested in military matters—particularly fort construction, since you are an engineer. You know about the recent trouble out there with the aircraft gun-bases?"

"Yes. I've been reading about that in the papers—hey! You don't mean—" Renny looked at the demolished instruments and cases in the laboratory. "Holy cow!"

Doc said, "You and Long Tom might go to Fort Atlantic immediately. You will investigate the gun-base trouble that has been featured in the newspapers—and note the fact that Rockaway Beach is very near Fort Atlantic. That may mean something."

"Where will you be, Doc?" Long Tom asked.

"Washington."

Doc entered a queer-looking car which traveled inside a pneumatic tube—dubbed the "flea run" by hairy Monk. This device was an underground shortcut that carried passengers to the water-front hangar of Doc Savage in a matter of moments.

Doc rolled a small speed plane to the landing stage located adjacent to the Hudson River, and some minutes later, he was in the air and pointing the nose of the ship toward Washington. The plane was capable of making three hundred miles an hour, which meant hardly more than an hour should be needed for the trip to Washington —but it took longer than that.

Flying over Chesapeake bay, Doc had some rather strange trouble.

Because there were low clouds over the Chesapeake, the bronze man had brought the plane down to less than a thousand feet; and in order to keep on the radio beam in case the ceiling clamped down, he had headed in close to shore. He had been riding the radio beam ten minutes or so when the trouble struck.

First, it touched the ship itself—something like an invisible hand seemed to clutch the wing tips, then shake them violently, as a mastiff might waggle a small terrier. One moment the plane was flying smoothly; the next it was a wild, weaving thing apparently trying to shake itself apart.

Next, the bronze giant experienced a peculiar trembling sensation in his own body—his chest seemed to tighten; his ears hurt; abruptly it felt as if his great muscles were being shaken from his frame.

There was nothing that could be seen! The fast plane was out of control while Doc Savage, with will power and strength, was trying to fight off the queer vibrating attack long enough to think of a way out of the predicament. The plane was going into a plunging dive; it would be only seconds until it lost all altitude.

Beads of perspiration stood on the bronze man's metallic features as, struggling against the rippling sensation all through his body, he partially righted the plane. Then he saw the right wing—the wing was shaking itself loose. In a few seconds it would rip free from the fuselage and the plane would be a tumbling, unmanageable death ship.

And as abruptly as the unseen, fantastic phenomenon had gripped the ship, it was gone. But too late; already the left wing was doubling slowly in the middle.

Beside the bronze man in the cockpit was a folded parachute; he always carried the safety device. Seemingly unmindful of the plane's zigzag course, of the fact that it was tumbling toward the river, he yanked the harness over his back and shoulders. Then he threw himself clear of the ship, waited the usual ten seconds with a grip on the rip-cord ring, then yanked. A scant few hundred feet below was water and land; he was near the shore line.

A few hundred feet above a scraggly beach, the chute opened and checked the bronze man's downward plunge. He landed in knee-deep water close to the shore, waded out on ground, surrounded by pale darkness. Doc freed himself from the harness, gathered up the chute and carried it with him as he climbed out of the water.

He concealed the parachute in bushes on shore. Then he turned to stare out over the dark, wide river.

Barely discernible in the mist were the running lights, hull and masts of a small craft which resembled a bugeye-type oyster schooner. The vessel had made no attempt to come to the bronze man's aid; it was heading down the river. Doc Savage, on an impulse, decided not to let whoever was on that craft know that he had not met death in the plane.

The plane plunged somewhere out near the middle of the river. The schooner chugged away, and there was silence.

It was daylight when Doc Savage reached Washington. A farmer going to market took Doc into Baltimore; there a hired cab covered the forty miles to the capital in close to forty minutes. The sun had turned very bright.

Doc phoned his New York headquarters. Renny and Long Tom were not there—evidently they had gone out on Long Island, but a robot machine, one of the bronze man's scientific devices, recorded the message. The mechanical voice of the contrivance made a preliminary speech, saying, *"This is the office of Clark Savage, Jr. There is no one here but you may talk and your message will be mechanically recorded. It will be delivered upon the return of someone to this office."*

Doc spoke for the recording device, leaving word for either Renny or Long Tom to bring another of his planes down to Washington. He explained that the one he was using had been lost.

Doc then proceeded to the downtown hotel where Monk and Ham were stopping. At the desk, a sleepy room clerk looked up—Doc was attired in a trench coat—and stared abruptly. Many persons knew Doc Savage by sight; this particular man did not, but he was awed by the bronze man's size and strange flake-gold eyes.

"I . . . ah . . . is there something—"

"You have two gentlemen stopping here, Mr. Mayfair and Mr. Brooks. Are they in?"

"You are—"

"Savage—Clark Savage."

"Word was left for you to go right up. Room fourteen-twelve."

Doc nodded, walked to the elevators and a moment later was let out on the fourteenth floor; he proceeded down a carpeted hallway, paused before the door of fourteen-twelve. The bronze man, ready to knock, suddenly paused with his hand inches from the door. He stood listening.

Behind the panel of the heavy door, there had been the sound of a low cough—a woman's cough.

Doc Savage used care not to make a sound, turned the knob until he learned the room was unlocked, then opened the door a crack. Light was turned on inside the room. He eased the door open wider. At first, he saw no one, only a dresser, desk, suitcases upon a stand, shaded bridge lamp. He stepped quietly inside.

The woman said brightly, "Well, mercy me, it's about time you got here!"

She was about the homeliest female the bronze man had ever seen.

She was middle-aged, if one wanted to be generous. She wore an old-fashioned black dress hinting of many petticoats beneath; her black shoes buttoned high up her ankles; her black straw hat had a straight, wide brim. She was dumpy. She had a face rather startlingly like a Great Dane dog.

"Well, my! I was just saying it was about time you got here."

"There must be a mistake."

"No mistake," the woman said. "Doc Savage, aren't you?"

"That's right."

"You'd better get busy then."

"Eh?"

"Mercy me, yes! Those two assistants of yours—that Monk and the one called Ham—well, they're in a mess of trouble."

Doc Savage thought he had entered the wrong room by mistake; he changed his mind.

"They didn't mention you, Miss—"

"Nanny Hanks."

The woman used her large, unshapely hands to smooth

her dress. She smiled; it was hard to tell whether the smile was something cheerful, or a grimace.

"They're chasing after that woman, Annabel Lynn, and she's got them all tangled up and chasing wild geese."

Doc's unusual eyes sharpened. "Just who are you?"

For answer, the woman took something from a large, old-fashioned handbag that she held on her lap. It was a small black case, and from the case she took a card, which she passed to the bronze man.

He saw in a glance that the card bore the emblem of the U. S. Secret Service, identifying the bearer as one Nanny Hanks, an operative. The bronze man's eyebrows raised a trifle. He fingered the identification card a moment, then passed it back.

Nanny Hanks said, "Don't let my looks fool you. I want to warn you about this Annabel Lynn. She's got one young man involved already—a chap named Warren Allen, an Englishman. And now she's after Monk and Ham."

Doc smiled. "In other words, you don't like her?"

The homely woman bristled. "Do you know what I think she really is?"

"What?"

"A foreign secret agent! And somehow she's connected with this Fort Atlantic trouble. You know—where the anti-aircraft gun foundations disintegrated."

"Do you know where Monk and Ham are now?"

Nanny Hanks nodded. "That's why I was wating for you. I know that they telephoned you tonight. I can show you where they are—or, at least, tell you how to get there."

"Suppose we do that," Doc suggested.

Nanny Hanks stood up, shook out the folds of her rather comical black dress and stepped briskly toward the hall door. "I have an angle of my own to investigate on this thing. But I'll tell you where I think they took Monk and Ham. I'll get in touch with you later."

"You can't go with me?"

"No. Sorry."

"I'm sorry, too. Where are Monk and Ham?"

"Out near the U. S. Soldiers' Home. There is a reservoir nearby, and a woods, and you look for an old workshed. They're there."

"Why are they there?"

"I don't know. I guess that silly Annabel decoyed them there."

"Can you give me any more information about this mystery?"

"No. Haven't any more."

Out on the street, they parted, and the dumpy, homely woman hurried down the block and turned the corner.

Two cabs were at the stand near the hotel entrance; Doc hailed one hack, gave the driver orders to let him out near the U. S. Soldiers' Home.

After the cab pulled away from the curb, Nanny Hanks came back from around the corner and stood watching the taxi as it disappeared down the street.

"That," she remarked, "should settle several things."

Chapter VII

RESERVOIR RENDEZVOUS

The cab in which Doc Savage was riding ran north to the outskirts of Washington. Near the Soldiers' Home he left the cab, told the driver not to wait, and walked toward a parklike woods which surrounded the reservoir. The woods were thick, deep, shaded, on a morning that was already starting to get hot. Doc Savage followed a path that bordered a steep embankment, partially concealed by trees.

Nanny Hanks had said there would be a workshed.

He walked for some time, but did not pick up any sign of a workshed; he climbed a bank and, still protected by low trees, looked out over the placid, clear water of the reservoir.

To the right, down near more woods at one end of the lake, he saw a small stone building; it appeared to be a place where supplies for the reservoir might be stored. There seemed to be no one about.

Shielded by the trees, Doc proceeded silently toward the shed. He could hear a pump working somewhere; the sound apparently came from some other building farther along the tree-lined embankment bordering the reservoir. There was no indication that anyone was in the shed.

The heavy door could be fastened with a padlock; the padlock hung, unlatched, on the hasp. The door stood ajar.

There was a dank, earthy smell to the place—and the sound of pumping was louder. At first, after the outdoors sunlight, it was hard to see clearly; Doc made out tools stacked against walls of the stone building. From a coat pocket, he took a flashlight, shot white glare around the small room. There was nothing of consequence except another door, also open, across the room.

Stone steps led downward. The sound of a pump working was much louder now. The steps ended in a tunnel that led underground, probably a passageway that led to a valve gate beneath the reservoir.

Doc was on the point of turning back when something caught his eye. He centered the light ray on the open doorway above the steps. The thing that had attracted his attention was a piece of cloth, a bit of fabric caught on the roughness of the door frame.

The bronze man pulled the bit of cloth loose, studied it beneath the flashlight glow. He noted that it was a specimen of dark, expensive cloth that might have come from a full-dress suit. The material was of very expensive weave, imported, rather rare. Doc's flake-gold eyes became thoughtful.

Ham owned a dozen full-dress suits made with just such expensive fabric.

Doc went down the stairs, but more cautiously now, not using the flashlight. He felt his way. The tunnel was long and straight, led downward; the walls were cold and damp, the air dank. There was no sound save the throbbing of the distant pump, growing louder with nearness. The tunnel finally ended in another small room. Doc stepped carefully inside, shot the light glow around.

The pump noise seemed to come from a grating set in the center of the cement floor. Doc started over to take a look—and the door through which he had entered slammed shut.

Doc leaped, caught hold of the dog-arm that was used for opening the heavy door; it would not budge. Then his sensitive nostrils caught something else. Odor! A hissing sound became audible. Whitish vapor began seeping beneath the door; it spread rapidly filling the small chamber.

Doc held his breath and fought the door. But he could not hold his breath forever, and the gas kept coming. He tried the grating. Steel, and fastened down.

He staggered about for a while, knees sagging until he folded to the hard flooring. He lay very still, hands beneath his face.

For long moments, there was silence. In the ceiling of the underground room was a small vent, which probably was the base of an air shaft that led above ground. Slowly the white vapor floated toward the vent opening, until the room was clear.

The heavy door through which the bronze man had entered opened and two men came cautiously into the room, guns ready in their fists. Last to come—he did not enter until his men had made sure that the bronze giant was completely out—came Ambrose, Ambrose of the big ears, the face that was brutally ugly.

Ambrose said, "You see, it takes a system. If you guys had jumped this bronze fellow like you did the two called Ham and Monk, you'd be candidates for a nice pine box. The gas was a bright idea."

"You sure the gas was good, Ambrose?"

The battered-faced leader grinned. "Doc Savage will be out for a week." Ambrose, it seemed, was the sort of man who got highly pleased with his own ideas.

Someone asked, "Where's sourpuss?"

"You mean Nanny Hanks?"

"Yeah."

"She'll be around. She fooled Savage, didn't she? That old wren is goin' to do us a lot of good."

Ambrose gave a grimace that was supposed to be a smile. "You sure that Monk and Ham are tied tight enough that they couldn't get away?"

One of the men nodded.

"Yeah—and lucky we caught 'em," he said. The speaker frowned. "But why hold them any longer?" He gave Doc's silent form a significant look. "I thought we was gonna take care of them two just like we are him?"

"We are!" Ambrose grinned. "But the boss wants to talk to that lawyer, the one called Ham. Thinks maybe Ham can say just how far Doc Savage got toward knowing what is going on—and whether Savage told anybody anything that will make us trouble."

Someone said, "The quicker we get it all over with, the better!"

Ambrose stepped across the room and unlocked the grating and yanked at a valve-lever below. Immediately sounds of the pump became more labored. There was a gurgling sound.

Almost immediately, water started to surge up out of the hole which the grating had closed. It came rapidly, soon eddying around their feet!

Ambrose ran toward the door, the only exit from the small stone-walled room. They had put their guns away. It was then that the bronze man came up off the floor, very much alive.

Doc Savage lunged into the group, moved with such whipping speed that Ambrose and his men knew several seconds of startled bewilderment.

Earlier, when first folded face-down in the floor, Doc had flicked into his mouth a capsule of a type which he always carried in his vest pocket, a capsule containing chemicals with an oxygen base that enabled him to refrain from breathing the gas-filled air until the place was clear.

The fight in the small stone-walled room was one-sided. The giant bronze man was a master of juju and several other forms of jujitsu, as well as the plain dockwalloper kind of fighting.

Quarters were too close for gun-play. Ambrose ducked, got clear. Doc Savage grabbed the necks of another pair. Using a carefully scientific pressure of his corded, metallic fingers, Doc worked on nerve centers in the necks of the two struggling men, so that soon thereafter they became unconscious.

Meantime, Ambrose himself did a quick fadeout, going through the door.

Carrying his two unconscious victims, Doc set out in pursuit of Ambrose. From far ahead, through the passage-way, came the echoes of pounding feet; Ambrose, it was evident, had almost reached the outside, through the work-shed.

Doc Savage ran along the tunnel-like passageway, up the

flight of steps, through the upper room and out into the small clearing in the woods, where warm morning sunlight hammered down through the trees. There was no one in sight.

Faintly to his ears came the sounds of someone running through the woods at some distance. Doc dumped the two prisoners in the shack—they could hardly get away while senseless—and set out silently in that direction. He ran, powerful leg muscles carrying him along a pathway that must have taken Ambrose several moments to follow. It led downhill, came out upon a dusty woods road. Somewhere around a curve ahead, a car motor started up, making loud sounds in the stillness of the trees and quiet morning. Doc leaped forward, dived beneath some foliage, emerged on a road.

A man was backing the car out onto the road from where it had been hidden beneath low-hanging branches. The car had one passenger, Ambrose, in the rear.

Windows in the sedan were open against the heat; Doc Savage saw this much and his hand flicked to his coat pocket, came out with a small grenade. Deftly, the bronze man flicked the grenade toward one of the open car windows. Immediately choking black smoke filled the car, puffing out of the windows and even enveloped the car itself in a fuzzy black ball.

Someone yelled, "Hey! What the hell! I can't see to drive!"

Doc jumped forward, yanked open a door of the car, grabbed a neck in the engulfing darkness. He got the driver. The victim let out a yelp. He had no idea what had grabbed him in the black smoke. They struggled. The man made desperate attempts to reach his shoulder holster. But as he was dragged from the car, he suddenly lost all interest in everything—Doc had lost patience and used a fist to change the shape of the man's jaw somewhat.

Ambrose, in the rear, was confused in the black smoke. "It . . . it's Doc Savage! Slug him, you fools!"

The suggestion came a little too late—Ambrose himself was seized. Doc yanked Ambrose from the seat, and one of the bronze man's hands moved swiftly and put a hypo needle into the arm of the leader. Shortly thereafter, Ambrose became stupefied, as if thoroughly drunk, which was caused by the truth serum that had been in the hypo needle.

But Ambrose did not even know the name of the person who employed him—at least, the truth serum didn't bring it out of him. Orders, it seemed, came by coded message. Payment for his activities was received by telegraphic money order.

"I know," Doc reflected grimly, "only one thing. A girl named Annabel Lynn tried to reach us. Ambrose was not sure that Annabel Lynn had not reached us. The girl knows something that is apparently of great importance."

Ambrose had been a distinct disappointment. Doc used the nerve-pressure manipulation of his fingers on his victim's neck, put Ambrose to sleep, piled both men back into the car, and climbed behind the wheel, set out down the woods road. Shortly, the dusty byway emerged onto a turnpike that skirted the extensive Soldiers' Home.

Fifteen minutes later Doc delivered the unconscious men to a local police precinct, where Doc was quickly recognized; the bronze man merely explained that he had been attacked by the thugs, and only desired that they be held for questioning. He left directions for locating the pair at the workshed, and stated he would return later.

He said nothing of a girl named Annabel Lynn; or that these men might somehow be connected with her, nor did he mention Fort Atlantic or Rockaway Beach, or the collapse of a corner of the Treasury Building, or any of the rest of the strange affair.

He merely left the men in charge of the precinct captain. A police prowl car and driver were placed at the bronze man's disposal for the trip back to the downtown hotel where Monk and Ham had been stopping.

Some distance up the street from the hotel, a small coupé was parked. The woman seated behind the wheel—she had incredibly homely features—saw Doc Savage enter the hotel.

Nanny Hanks, the woman in the coupé, watched the bronze giant out of sight in the hostelry. She said:

"Well, mercy me—I'll be damned! We can't have him messing with this thing!"

Chapter VIII

WASHINGTON INTERVIEW

It was noon when Doc Savage again returned to the hotel where Monk and Ham had a room. At the desk, Doc learned that neither of his aids had yet returned; he asked if there had been any message from New York, or the arrival of any of his assistants from there, but the clerk had no messages.

Doc became thoughtful. He had left word on the mechanical-recorder device at his headquarters for either Renny or Long Tom to bring down another plane. The assignment he had given them to visit Fort Atlantic should have been covered by now, or they should have checked with the office. It was a little strange that neither had contacted him.

He left a message for Monk and Ham, should they return, and went back to the police car. The driver was reading a newspaper which had just come out, and he pointed to headlines and exclaimed:

"Say, look at this, will you?"

The headline read:

U. S. ARMY'S
NEWEST GUN
COLLAPSES

Baltimore Md.—It was learned from reliable sources that a new 155-millimeter gun, with a range of about fifteen miles, has collapsed on its ten-wheel rubber-tired mobile base at Fort James. The gun, weighing more than fifteen tons, had been temporarily placed at the fort at the channel entrance to Baltimore.

Doc intently scanned the news item. The fort mentioned was on the Chesapeake—and not far from where he had crashed in his plane during the night—after the craft had been so strangely seized by that shaking phenomenon.

The item continued:

It seems that a guard, stationed on the grounds where the new gun was being kept, discovered the queer state of affairs just after dawn. Army officials are releasing little information, but it is understood that the gun was found to be little more than a pile of loose iron fragments and metallic powder.

"Strange, ain't it?" the police-car driver asked, when Doc Savage had finished reading.

Doc's answer puzzled the cop.

"Perhaps not as strange as it seems," Doc said thoughtfully. "Perhaps it begins to get very clear."

Doc Savage seldom divulged his ideas; if he saw any connection between the antiaircraft gun-base trouble at Fort Atlantic, and this newest gun-collapse mystery near Baltimore, he said nothing, it being his custom to say little until he had a complete solution to a mystery. He said, "Drive to the war-department building."

The police driver slipped the car into gear, and ten minutes later the bronze man was going up the steps to the great edifice that housed the state, war and navy departments. To a receptionist in the lobby he said quietly, "It is quite urgent that I see the secretary of war."

For a moment, the woman looked as if she was going to say, "You can't just walk in here and get to see the secretary of war." But when Doc added, "The name is Clark Savage, Jr.," the receptionist swallowed hastily and dialed—not the assistant secretary to the secretary—but the secretary of war rear admiral himself. "Clark Savage, Jr., to see you," she advised.

Shortly, a man in uniform appeared at the receptionist's desk, smiled at Doc, said quietly, "Right this way, sir." The woman stared after the bronze giant. She was impressed, for no one in Washington could have gained quicker admittance to the head of the war department.

Had the receptionist seen the room into which the bronze man was ushered, she would have been more impressed. It was a long, somber-looking place that looked like a director's board room, and Doc Savage recognized many of the men seated solemnly around the table—high-ranking officials of the war and navy departments. Expressions on their faces indicated they had not gathered to swap jokes.

Rear Admiral Harvey Benton—a short, slender man with alert, sharp eyes—came forward and shook hands with the bronze man, and he said, "It must be important business that brings you to Washington?"

Others stood up and nodded to Doc. The work of Doc Savage was well known here in Washington; often he had been called in to help various governmental departments when some particularly knotty problem cropped up.

Doc came to the point quickly.

He said, "You quite recently had a mysterious building collapse here in Washington—the Treasury Building."

One of the men seated at the table said, "We are convinced that it was a bold, reckless attempt to rob a part of the treasury. Luckily, police and other guards arrived in time to scare the crooks off." The speaker gave a forced smile.

Doc nodded, but his expression did not indicate whether he agreed or disagreed with the man's statement.

"A new gun base at Fort Atlantic, located at a vital spot on Long Island, has been found worthless."

There was an uncomfortable stir among the men seated around the table. Someone said with forced easiness, "Contractor trouble! Too much sand, not enough cement."

Doc made no comment on that, although he knew the contractor had an enviable record for reliable work. He continued: "And now, early this morning, the army's newest long-range gun collapsed. This, too, happened at a vital point along the Atlantic coast."

The silence got electric—somewhat like the quiet in a death chamber just before a man is electrocuted. A chair scraped on the polished floor; someone coughed.

Doc said, "Has it occurred to you gentlemen that there might be a connection between these incidents?"

It was Rear Admiral Benton who spoke up. "We have already discussed such possibilities. And we have learned that the whole thing was merely coincidence."

He gave Doc a big grin—a grin he worked hard to make. "You had something in mind, sir?"

For a moment, Doc's strange flake-gold eyes stirred restlessly. "This thing might be even bigger than *you* think," he said. "And incidentally, you're not fooling me."

"You're having a pipe dream, Savage," a man said.

Doc gave a brief smile. "Perhaps I am wrong. Thank you, gentlemen, for the interview."

Doc turned, and there was a forced air of this-is-just-a-little-social-gathering as he went out.

The bronze man had said nothing of the strange vibration that had hit himself and his plane somewhere over the Chesapeake, of the demolished instruments in his laboratory, or of the mystery as to why unknown individuals were suddenly interested in killing himself and some of his men. He was a little angry—a mood in which he rarely permitted himself to fall. He had never forced his services upon any organization. People in trouble sought him; but in this case he had been trying to forestall a menace that was still vague and unknown.

In the room which Doc had left, excitement broke loose, many men talking at once. One man barked, "You see, even *he* suspects!" And another yelled, "The President is seeing us at four o'clock. Gentlemen, there is need for action. Every scientific device the government owns must be used to locate whatever *thing* is causing this damage!"

A third man groaned, "The newspapers have got to be warned. If someone hits on what we suspect is the *real* truth, my friends, there might be panic!"

Outside the building, Doc Savage climbed back in the police prowl car that had been placed at his disposal.

The driver said, "Know what?"

Doc looked at the burly cab driver. "Eh?"

"I wish they would follow *me* around."

"I fail to get your meaning."

"Dame following you!"

The driver pointed down the street, to where a small coupé was parked. He added, "I noticed that car in the rear-view mirror a couple times when we were driving up here. It pulled up there ahead after you went inside, and she's been there ever since. She's been waiting for you to come out."

Doc said, "We might check on that."

"How?" the cop driver queried.

"By seeing if she follows us again."

"Good idea."

The driver put the prowl car in gear and eased down the street at ordinary speed. Then he stepped on the gas, did some fancy cutting in and out of traffic, around various corners, reached another main thoroughfare and slowed down again. He looked in the mirror.

"You see? She's still on our trail."

Doc nodded. He said, "Mind if I take the wheel a moment?"

The cop slid over and Doc took his place. What the prowl-car driver learned about the game of four-wheeled hide-and-seek in the next ten minutes was breathtaking. They finally ended up on a busy thoroughfare in midtown, where Doc drove carefully once again.

He turned the wheel over to the driver. "Let her pick up your trail again, then lose her if you can. Keep her interested in trailing you. I get off here—just slow down."

Doc stepped from the running board as the cop swung in close to the curb. When the officer looked back later, Doc Savage had disappeared. He had stepped into a taxicab that had been parked at the corner. So quiet was the bronze man's entry into his hack, the cabby looked startled.

Doc said, "Wait here. There is a car I want you to follow."

Later, the small coupé came swiftly along the street. Its driver had again spotted the police prowl car and was following at a discreet distance.

Doc instructed, "Follow that coupé."

He had gotten a look at the coupé's occupant—it was Nanny Hanks.

Doc Savage's brief turn at the wheel of the squad car must have been instructive to the police driver. For he showed sudden improvement in the hare-and-hound business—before they had gone two miles, he had lost Nanny Hanks and her coupé.

The homely-faced woman slowed down and seemed to be on the verge of parking, then she swung down a side street and stepped on the gas. Apparently she had decided upon some other move. The shift in plans pleased the bronze man; to the cab driver, he said, "Now follow her. Try not to make it obvious."

Doc Savage, having reversed the procedure of being pursued, and being now the pursuer, followed a trail that led away from the downtown section and out Pennsylvania Avenue until they had crossed the Anacosta River. There, Nanny Hanks swung her coupé right, and soon it was apparent that they were following the highway to Bolling Field, the big army airport.

The midday traffic was fairly heavy, and there was nothing particularly noticeable about the cab trailing the coupé; there were many cabs on the road.

At a large gate to Bolling Field, Nanny Hanks stopped a moment, showed something to the guard—evidently she was exhibiting a pass, for Nanny Hanks was quickly admitted.

Doc said, "Drop me here." He paid the cabby, walked up to the gate watchman and himself handed the man a small card he carried as an honorary member of the Intelligence Service. The guard stared at the card and then at the bronze man. "Mr. Savage," he said quickly. "Go right in."

Doc saw that Nanny Hanks had parked her car far down the field, near a hangar that was set somewhat apart from the rest. Doc walked in that direction; the homely-looking woman had been inside the hangar for some moments by the time he reached the spot. He heard a heated argument taking place. Familiar voices. Monk and Ham! They were apparently in another of their frequent wrangles.

Monk was saying in his small voice, "Listen, shyster, she don't ride with *me!*"

Ham, as dapper as usual with his sword-cane and a snappy tropical-worsted suit, grimaced.

He said wearily, "You hairy mistake, wasn't it her influence that got the commander here to let us have an Army plane? And she knows about Annabel Lynn. What more do you want?"

Doc walked inside.

"Doc!"

Both were pleased at the sight of the bronze man.

"Strange about our New York headquarters, Doc," Ham said. "We've been trying to reach you or anybody else up there, and we can't get an answer."

Doc nodded, glanced toward a fast-looking army cabin job standing in the hangar and said, "There seems to be some argument?"

Ham explained, "A woman named Nanny Hanks, a government operative, has given us a lead to the whereabouts of Annabel Lynn."

"Who is Annabel Lynn?"

"A girl who is in trouble, and who has some sort of information for you, Doc. That's all we know about her, except that we can't locate her."

"And your present squabble is about—"

Ham pointed at Monk. "Well, goofus here, he's worried because Nanny Hanks fell for him. Maybe she is kind of hard to look at, but she's been helpful—"

"Helpful?" Hairy Monk cut in. "She scares five years off my life every time I look at her."

Just then a door opened across the huge hangar. Nanny Hanks came from what was evidently an office, spied the bronze man and hurried over.

"My, my! Doc Savage!" The homely woman's face suddenly looked worried as she frowned at the big bronze man. "You know," she said quickly, "I made a mistake about that reservoir hide-out."

"Mistake?"

Nanny Hanks nodded. "Yes. I thought Monk and Ham had been taken there. I did not mean to send you into such danger."

Doc made no comment. From what he had overheard

back at the reservoir, apparently Nanny Hanks was working with Ambrose and his men. She had most certainly led Doc into a trap, but now here she was again, apparently trying to help Doc.

The bronze man decided to give the homely little woman more rope—but the next moment, she made a statement that made him wonder whether she was fool or sage.

Nanny Hanks said, "I know where you can find Annabel Lynn. Also that man Warren Allen. He is sweet on her, and he followed her."

"Followed her where?"

"To New York!" Then the woman suddenly came over and touched Doc's arm. "Also, there is something else!"

Doc waited, said nothing.

"We'd better get to that bridge," Nanny Hanks said worriedly.

"What bridge?"

"The new bridge over the East River at New York," Nanny Hanks said tensely. "Maybe we can stop it. But we'll have to hurry!"

"Stop what?"

Nanny Hanks gave him a strange stare. "That's all I know—just something is maybe going to happen to that bridge. Don't forget—it's the new bridge."

Something in the stout woman's tone said that she was not making idle remarks. She seemed to be a storehouse of information; the bronze man got the feeling that she knew more than she was telling.

"You wish to go with us?" he asked.

"That was my idea," Nanny Hanks said, and nodded.

Doc made a decision. To Nanny Hanks, he said, "It might be a good idea if we all got started then."

A fast military plane—the ship which the army was loaning them—was wheeled out of the hangar by field attendants. Monk tried desperately to avoid Nanny Hanks and her ugly face, but Nanny grabbed the hairy chemist's hand and said cooingly, "Gracious! Planes simply frighten me to death! You will sort of look after poor little me, won't you?"

Monk scowled, and Doc, climbing into the cockpit, watched the incident with thoughtful eyes. Nanny Hanks was either very smitten with the fabulously homely Monk —or playing some very clever game.

Chapter IX

MANHATTAN MENACE

Doc Savage handled the controls on the flight back toward New York, while Ham, the lawyer of their organization, rode in the cockpit beside Doc, this making it necessary for homely Monk to ride in the cabin with the woman who was fully as homely as himself.

Monk sat and glared at the earth that passed far below. Nanny Hanks looked fondly at the hairy chemist and tried to smile sweetly at him. Monk's personal opinion—it was not an unfair opinion, either—was that Nanny Hank's smile was something to crack a mirror.

Nanny Hanks said, "You must be a terribly strong man. Er—I've always admired strong men."

Monk tried to change the subject. "The reason Doc's takin' you with us," he said, "is because you know about Annabel Lynn."

A so-this-must-be-heaven expression came into the chemist's small eyes, and he said dreamily, "Boy, now there's a girl for you!"

Nanny Hanks grimaced wryly. "Humph!" she snorted.

"You poor fellow! Like most men, I see you are a pushover for a pretty face. I was hoping you would be different."

Monk glanced at Nanny Hanks and frowned. "What's wrong with that girl?" he demanded.

"Annabel Lynn is a spy," Nanny Hanks said, gripping her large, old-fashioned purse tightly as the plane hit bumpy going.

"I don't believe it," Monk yelled.

"You'll find out," his ugly cabin companion yelled back at him. "If you think that Lynn hussy is honest, you need someone to take care of you!"

"He's always needed a keeper," Ham called back unkindly.

Monk growled something to himself, turned his back, got his jaw settled down on his big hands and glared out the cabin window. Pretty girls, he liked. But a woman as homely as this—

And in the cockpit, Doc was questioning dapper Ham about exactly what had happened in Washington; he was learning more about Annabel Lynn and about the young Englishman named Warren Allen, who seemed to be crazy about her.

Ham finished, "Apparently this Lynn girl was afraid of these same birds who captured us temporarily. I'm certain she can explain something about antiaircraft gun-base trouble and the Treasury Building collapse. And now— somehow—this Nanny Hanks learned that Annabel Lynn is again on the way to our New York headquarters. I don't get this Nanny Hanks. I can't make her out."

"She claims to be a Secret Service agent."

"Did you ever hear of the Secret Service having such an agent?"

They had been flying at ten thousand feet, above scattered clouds in the west. The sun was dropping toward the horizon in a red glare. Ahead, Doc picked up the lightship stationed outside New York harbor. He started losing altitude.

He said, "Perhaps you should know more about this Nanny Hanks."

Ham gave the bronze man a puzzled look. "Know what?" he asked.

With one hand off the controls, Doc passed the lawyer a small card. It was the identification card Nanny Hanks had shown Doc back at the hotel room in Washington. Apparently, as far as Nanny Hanks knew, Doc had returned that card to her at the hotel.

But the bronze man had switched the card for one of the same size he had carried in his pocket; he had wanted to keep the woman's card for a while, for reasons of his own.

Now he handed Ham a second card, one that identified himself as an honorary member of the Secret Service.

"Compare them," Doc said.

Ham did so, said, "Well, they're the same. Nanny Hanks showed me her card earlier—"

"Look more closely."

The lawyer gave the bronze man a sharp look, then scrutinized the cards again. "The United States seal is different! Not much, but with the two cards together this way, I can detect some difference."

Doc said, "Nanny Hank's card is a forgery."

Ham gulped. "Then she's lying! She's not in the Secret Service. Why in the dickens did you bring her along?"

Doc was busy guiding the plane down over lower New York Bay. He said quietly, "It might be a good idea to have her around, so we can watch her."

A few moments later the plane passed over the Narrows —the entrance to New York harbor—and Doc flew fairly low now. Tugs, ferries, steamships moved back and forth below them, leaving long trails of wake. Doc tooled the army plane up the Hudson, past the upper Bay, past the water-front warehouse-hangar that he maintained. He swerved to cross upper Manhattan.

He was, they realized, flying toward the new East River bridge.

Ham said, "Maybe the rear admiral and those other officers were right, Doc. I mean what they said about this Fort Atlantic trouble and that gun falling apart down near Baltimore. It *could* have been coincidence."

Ham turned to stare out a window. They were well north of the harbor and approaching the great bridge that connected New York City with Long Island on the east. Ham kept staring, and he said oddly, "Doc, there's something funny about that bridge—"

And at that moment, hairy Monk reared up in the cabin.

His little eyes were wild-looking, and he cried shrilly, "Doc! That bridge! It's falling down!"

The bronze man had already seen. Hands steady on the controls, metallic features grim, he let the plane drop swiftly in order that they might get a closer view.

One end of the vast bridge seemed to sag down farther on one of the great "anchors" at the New York end. It gave another jerk, and the bridge collapsed against the mammoth mooring.

Doc throttled the plane motors. Over the soft rush of the plane through the air, they could hear a tremendous grinding and tearing sound made by steel against cement and rock. Thousands of tons were ripping loose at the New York approach to the mighty structure.

It was as though a giant fist was pressing down on one end of the bridge, snapping supports, pulverizing the hundreds of tons of concrete that locked one end of the bridge to the embankment of the river.

Ham and Monk stared speechlessly. Homely Nanny Hanks, crowding her face into the cockpit, said oddly, "Dear me! We're too late!" She looked at Doc, said tensely, "I think you had better call Washington!"

Doc Savage himself said nothing, but his flake-gold eyes were very thoughtful.

So excited were Monk and Ham that they had not heard Nanny Hanks' reference to calling Washington.

Doc abruptly lowered one wing, sent the plane in a long circle, turning back from the bridge as though he might have sensed danger.

Beneath them, on a boulevard that bordered the river edge, thousands of cars had stopped and people were climbing out of the machines to stare at this thing that had happened to the bridge.

The bridge itself looked like some giant Coney Island slide, lower at one end than at the other. Luckily, it had not dropped far enough to plunge into the river. Such cars as had been on it were jammed one against the other along its length. People had piled from the machines and were lined against the bridge rails. Some were already leaping into the water far below, fearing the bridge might collapse farther. There apparently had been no cars near the end that had collapsed when the actual damage occurred.

Then the vibration struck their plane—only the merest touch, as though they might have been merely brushed by the very edge of some fantastic, incarnate, ethereal monster. The plane shook from end to end for a moment.

Monk, Ham, Nanny Hanks were all hurled about.

The bronze man—he had experienced this incredible thing once before, over the Chesapeake—forced his great hands to be rock-steady on the controls. But the strange phenomenon lasted only a moment.

Doc brought the plane down fast for a landing near his water-front hangar; later they were climbing out inside the great warehouse-hangar. Doc said, "We may have an answer to this business as soon as we reach the lab."

When they reached the eighty-sixth floor headquarters of the bronze man, Doc left Monk and Nanny Hanks in the reception room, while he hurried into the laboratory. He had not explained his comment about having an answer to the bridge collapse and its connection, possibly, with the other happenings. First, he wanted to make certain of something.

He went directly to a complicated instrument which he had installed before flying to Washington. The apparatus was another seismograph for registering exact time of earth disturbances—an instrument similar to the one that had been shattered in his laboratory earlier.

Doc studied the chart in the sensitive machine. The seismoscope showed no time indication of an earth shock. It indicated nothing whatsoever.

No explosive blast, then, had demolished that bridge support.

Doc Savage made one more investigation—he mounted a narrow stairway, concealed in the laboratory walls, which led upward to the roof of the skyscraper. Atop the building was a dirigible mooring-mast, a device that was ornamental rather than practical, which thrust up another hundred feet into the air. A circular staircase led up inside this, and Doc reached the top.

Mounted here, at a point which put them farthest from the city noises, was a battery of aircraft-defense listener-locators. The complicated devices, utilizing super-sensitive parabolic microphones and amplifiers, were sensitive enough to detect the buzzing of a fly hundreds of feet distant.

Such sounds as the listeners received were recorded automatically on cylinders. Doc played back the recordings, listening intently to the sounds which had been recorded about the time—there was a time-indicating device in connection with the recorded cylinders—that the bridge had collapsed.

He found something that interested him, for he made a telephone call to the nearest army headquarters.

"I want a stratosphere plane," he said. "One which is capable of flying extremely high, and extremely fast. Complete oxygen equipment aboard."

"The ship will be waiting when you need it."

Doc returned to the reception room. Monk, seated in a deep chair, was scowling at Nanny Hanks, who was looking at the hairy chemist fondly. At least her attitude was one that was supposed to indicate a fond regard for Monk —although to Monk, it looked as if Nanny Hanks was trying to scare away a wolf. Monk looked at Doc and his lips moved.

"Gosh, what a homely morsel," Monk said. Doc read his lips.

Ham came in, and he was excited. Seeing Doc, he exclaimed, "That bridge disaster is having a weird effect on people, Doc! Everybody is keeping out of the subways. Hundreds are even getting out of town. They're afraid of the invisible monster."

Monk jumped up.

"*What?*" he yelled.

"They've got the idea something crushed that bridge," the well-dressed lawyer went on swiftly. "They say only something huge and invisible could have caused the bridge to fall down!"

Everyone looked at the bronze man. Doc said nothing.

"Maybe it was an earthquake?" Monk muttered.

Doc said, "There has been no earthquake."

Monk's small eyes were worried. "You mean," he piped, "that there's really a *thing* that causes that funny trembling feeling that hit us?"

"Exactly," said Doc.

"What is it?"

"That," Doc explained, "is what we had better be finding out before long." The bronze man had turned to Ham.

"You might," he suggested, "see if there has been any word from Renny or Long Tom."

Ham hurried to the library to see if there was any message on the special recording machine which Doc used to leave messages when no one was at headquarters. He returned shortly.

Ham's face was worried. "No message from Long Tom or Renny," he reported. He held out a slip of paper in his hand. "But there was this. I can't understand how it got here."

It was a hastily written note, in a woman's fine handwriting, and it read:

Doc Savage:
You must help me find my uncle. I have gone to Fort Watson, on Staten Island. Please hurry. There is so little time. My uncle is the key to this whole incredible thing.

Annabel Lynn

The phone in the reception room rang and Doc lifted the receiver. He listened, his face expressionless, as someone talked tensely on the other end of the line. After a while, when he hung up the receiver, his flake-gold eyes were animated.

"What was it?" Ham wanted to know.

Doc said, "First, you and Monk had better go to Staten Island and find Annabel Lynn." He nodded toward the stout little woman who claimed to be a Secret Service operative. "Take Nanny Hanks with you. You might also try and pick up some trace of Long Tom and Renny."

From the tone of Doc's vibrant voice, Ham knew there had been great urgency in the phone call. He asked again:

"Doc, what was that call—"

The bronze man gave Nanny Hanks a significant look, said, "It will not be necessary to get in touch with Washington. They have already called us."

Without further comment, Doc started toward the door. A moment later came the whining of cables as a high-speed elevator dropped the Man of Bronze toward his basement garage.

As Monk left with Ham and Nanny Hanks, Monk whispered, "Blazes, this old gal gives me a complex!"

Monk looked worried all the way down in the elevator cab. Still trying to think of some way in which to divert the homely woman's attentions from himself, he suggested to Ham, "You get the car. I'll wait outside the building with . . . with the goblin, here."

Ham departed to get the car.

Following his policy of ignoring Nanny Hanks, Monk turned his back on her and stood at the curb. Ham finally drove up in one of the bronze man's cars. Monk started to pile in. Nanny Hanks had disappeared.

Chapter X

THE MAN WHO WOULDN'T TALK

Doc Savage parked his car near Miller Field, the U. S. army airport outside New York City, and found the officer in charge.

"You have the stratosphere plane for which I asked?" the bronze man inquired.

The officer indicated a plane—largely streamlined motor cowling, with just a little wing—that stood on the tarmac. "There it is."

"Oxygen tanks?"

"Aboard. That ship will go higher than any other plane on earth. You should know. It was your design from which the thing was built. The ship holds the present altitude record. Not that particular ship, but one just like it."

Doc Savage was satisfied. He changed the subject, asking, "How many of the new type of listener-locator devices for spotting airplanes do you have?"

"More than the public imagines, probably," the officer said cautiously. "To tell you the exact figure, I would have to consult records."

"That is not important. The main thing is: How soon could you get them into action?"

"Ten minutes, I should say. We have all the listeners connected with short-wave radio, and the crews are frequently drilled for alarm duty."

"I may want you to use them on short notice," Doc said.

"To spot a plane for you, you mean?"

Instead of answering the query directly, Doc said, "The listening devices are equipped with telephonic headsets, are they not? So that the crew can distinguish the exact nature of any sounds that may be picked up for an altitude of as much as thirty thousand feet."

"That's right. The crews can listen with headsets."

"Good." The bronze man nodded. "If I need the services of the listeners, I will possibly be able to tell you exactly what kind of a sound to listen for."

"Then you don't want to use them to spot a plane?"

"What we're trying to spot," Doc Savage told him, "is a good deal more sinister than any plane."

Without elaborating on this rather mysterious remark, the bronze man walked to the plane. He was familiar with the type of craft, having created the basic designs for the ship. He noted that the instrument layout in the cockpit had been altered from his own layout, and improved, he was willing to admit.

A glance at the windsock over the hangars gave him wind direction—it would be necessary, in order to take off, to taxi across the field, turn, and come back. He operated the compressed air starter, got the big motor exploding slowly, then checked gauges and oxygen supply.

The cabin was a type that could be closed in entirely, hermetically sealed. Even so, a suit or oxygen helmet was necessary when flying at extremely high altitudes.

He gunned the motor, and the craft began moving across the tarmac.

A man came running toward the ship. He wore an army uniform, was in a great hurry. He climbed into the cabin apologetically.

"Awfully sorry," he said. "Got orders from Washington to send an observer along with you in this plane. We're frightfully embarrassed about it, but—well, orders are orders. My name is Philips." He extended his hand.

Doc shook hands with Philips, then they took the air, the plane lunging across the field pouring a drool of red sparks from exhaust stacks. Up . . . up . . . up. Five thousand, ten thousand, fifteen thousand feet. Doc handled the controls, kept busy watching gas and oil pressures, and preparing to compensate for the changes in atmospheric pressure.

When they hit thirty thousand feet altitude, if it had not been for the oxygen suits both men wore, they would have been unconscious. Almost six miles below, the island of Manhattan was an elongated smear of light in a world of blackness. The stratosphere plane, under Doc's guidance, lined out for Fort Watson, on Staten Island.

Doc was going to look into the summons he had received from Annabel Lynn—the note which had said her uncle was the key to the whole mystery.

Philips, the observer, turned around. Something about the assistant's eyes puzzled the bronze giant, for Philips seemed to be grinning.

"Nice test," he said. "You were merely testing the ship, weren't you?"

Doc nodded.

They kept dropping rapidly. Variation in air pressure was terrific; it meant constant regulating of release valves in the oxygen units, and it was much like the change in pressure encountered by a deep-sea diver.

At fifteen thousand feet, they were able to discard the artificial aid of oxygen.

Then Philips turned around and came toward Doc. His features were square, granite-hard, menacing; the man was no longer the young, pleasant-faced Philips. He was completely different.

But there was nothing strange about the evil glint in the man's cold eyes. The way he snaked his wiry form forward indicated he had no regard for his own life; showed suddenly that he was a fanatic, the type of person who leaps before police and hundreds of guards in order to assassinate a president. His eyes, the expression on his face, were all unnatural.

Philips had a gun in his fist. Doc Savage pulled himself up in the cockpit just as the bleak-eyed man raised the gun and fired. The man lifted his head and laughed wildly, but his mirth could not be heard above the propeller roar; instead, there was only the distorted talk-grin on his face.

Doc was thrown against the cockpit side by the impact of the pistol slug against his bullet-proof vest. Then he did a thing that took the would-be killer completely by surprise.

The bronze man immediately hurled himself forward. His sinewed hands gripped the gunman's shoulders and yanked the man forward. He got hold of the man holding the smoking gun. Doc gave a quick, short twist of the man's wrist—the fellow was wiry and powerful; surprise leaped into his eyes when he found himself so helpless in the bronze giant's grip—and the gun fell onto the cockpit floor boards. The man's face twisted in pain. His arm was useless, broken at the wrist. With his free hand, he made a clutch for the bronze man's throat.

Wind was screaming through the struts. The plane went into a slide-slip, then a spin, and Doc and his captive were hurled about in the cabin. Doc got his legs hooked beneath the cockpit instrument-panel, swung the other man partially into a seat, found nerve centers in the fellow's neck with his long, powerful fingers, and applied pressure so that the gunman became limp.

It was with some difficulty that the bronze man was able to support the stranger, to keep him from tumbling out of the seat, and fight to control the plane at the same time. The fast ship had gone out of control. It was only with rapid, trained effort that Doc Savage pulled it out of its falling-leaf downward plunge.

It was getting dark.

Doc picked up the field lights of the army airport, huge floods that lighted the long field from end to end. And off to one side were men waiting tensely, a "crash" car nearby. They seemed to be expecting a crack-up. Apparently they had discovered that Philips was an enemy in the plane with the man of bronze.

Doc Savage felt his chest gingerly. That gun blast against his ribs had been stunning, but not fatal—the chain-mesh bulletproof vests such as he and his aids often used were easily concealed beneath outer clothing. The bulletproof shields had more than once saved their lives, so they wore them continuously. They were not much heavier than an ordinary thick leather jacket, and far cooler.

Doc set the plane down on the field and taxied the ship up to a hangar. Army officials, mechanics, field guards came running to him. An ambulance followed.

Someone shouted, "We discovered that fellow who climbed into the ship was a fake right after you took off, sir! He knocked a gate guard out when the guard wouldn't let him in."

"It had to be something like that, I figured," Doc said. Then he turned back to the cockpit. The imposter, Philips, was stirring in the seat, slowly regaining consciousness.

Doc dragged Philips out, handed him over to waiting guards.

"We better question him," Doc said.

They took the passenger to the nearby field office. There, bleak-eyed Philips came entirely out of his stupor; Doc's nerve-paralyzing pressure on the man's neck had been only sufficient to keep the fellow helpless a short time.

The would-be killer glared at those assembled around him. He was holding his broken wrist, and there was baleful hate in his eyes as he looked at Doc.

The bronze man asked, "Who ordered you here? Who ordered you to kill me?"

The man continued to glare, said nothing.

From a special vest beneath his coat—an equipment vest that fitted neatly under his clothing—Doc took a small hypodermic syringe. The fake copilot's flying suit was removed. The ambulance attendant, at Doc Savage's instructions, rolled back the captive's sleeve.

Doc explained briefly, "Truth serum. It should make him talk."

He gave the surly-looking pilot the injection. The serum, while it worked more often than not, was not infallible in making close-mouthed captives reveal information. In this case, the most vital information needed was the name of the person or persons intent on eliminating Doc Savage, and the nature of the weird being, force or power—whatever it was—that was causing buildings to collapse.

"What is this trouble all about?" Doc asked.

The captive opened his mouth, trying not to speak. He

was trying to fight the effects of the drug which made him want to talk—the stuff wasn't working on him properly. Perspiration stood out on his brow. But something else showed in his eyes. Fear. Intense, stark fear.

Doc Savage was the first to notice it, and simultaneously he observed that the captive pilot shot a brief glance toward a small window in the room.

The bronze man whirled just as a shot crashed into the room.

The captive staggered, clawed air, then slowly folded to the floor, landing half on his side and half on his back, and a small gout of blood tumbled from the bullet hole in the center of his forehead. Almost immediately, the lights went out. Not only the lights within the office, but the big airport floodlights as well.

Instantly, there was confusion. Excited cries.

Everyone discovered this as they raced outside to seize the killer who had shot Philips. All they found was blackness and confusion. The gunman had escaped.

Doc thought back grimly and realized that he must have been close to learning the solution of a great many things; that accounted for Philips having been killed. Only for a small detail, a piece of instinctive precaution, Doc Savage would have perhaps received the same fate—he had been out of line with the window in the airfield office.

There was a great deal of dashing around, searching and asking questions, but it came to nothing.

Chapter XI

SCREAM IN THE NIGHT

Monk and Ham were becoming particularly interested in finding the attractive, regal-looking Annabel Lynn. Somewhere near the eastern shore of Staten Island, the two were walking. It was almost midnight, and intensely dark. They had left their car parked at the end of a road that led to a sandy stretch of deserted beach; they were now headed northward, toward the United States government reservation known as Fort Watson.

They were interested in finding a girl with gray-blue eyes, who was tall and slender and lovely, who, in well-dressed Ham's opinion—to say nothing of the opinion of Monk—was one of the most exquisite pieces of femininity he had ever encountered.

Off to the right lay the ocean, and through the darkness came the occasional, mournful note of a fog horn, a warning to liners entering the Narrows to New York that there was shoal near.

Monk and Ham pushed along, making noise for their own entertainment, for another half mile.

Finally a wire fence loomed up in the darkness, and on a pole embedded in the sand was a sign:

WARNING
U. S. GOVERNMENT
RESERVATION
KEEP OUT!

The two men ignored the warning and climbed through the wire.

Monk said gloomily: "I don't think Annabel Lynn is here. They don't allow women in these forts."

"I was thinking of that," agreed Ham. "Maybe there was something phony about that note at headquarters."

Then the scream came out of the darkness somewhere ahead, emanating from a spot where there was the vague outline of some massive structure above the beach, and the terrified yell came from there. And the outcry dispelled all thoughts the two aids might have had about there being no women allowed at the fort, for it was a girl's high-pitched, frantic cry that they were hearing.

They lunged forward now. Up the loose sand of the beach, climbing over rocks and an embankment that rose above the shore, the two raced toward the source of that outcry.

A high wall of part of the fort bulked before them. Last dying echoes of the girl's scream, like the last jangle of breaking glass, seemed to come from somewhere beneath this very wall, close ahead.

Monk, worried, barked, "You got a flashlight?"

Ham was already pulling a flashlight from his pocket. He thumbed it on, sent the white beam waving ahead, and the glare revealed a prisonlike wall on their left, with rough, stony ground underfoot.

A blond girl in a two-piece knitted suit was just lifting herself from her knees, where she seemed to have fallen on the stony ground below the fort wall. Her shapely, slim legs flashed in the glow of Ham's flashlight as she started running again, and her slender hand hovered near her throat in terror.

"Annabel!" Monk howled. "Annabel Lynn!"

Ham, always the more self-controlled of the two, drew

up short. He called to the tall blond girl, "Miss Lynn! It's the two Doc Savage men you met in Washington!"

After that, the girl halted in the flashlight glare, but seemed undecided as to which way to turn or what to do. Then she stumbled toward Monk and Ham holding out her slim hands, gasping "Oh, thank heavens!"

Ham caught the girl's hands, held them reassuringly as she trembled against him, while Monk glared wrathfully at the dapper lawyer.

Monk, not to be outdone in chivalry, grinned at the girl.

"Remember me?" the hairy chemist said hopefully. "I've been trying to help you ever since we made that appointment to meet in the restaurant in Washington."

For a moment, in her fright, the girl stared at Monk.

The girl began talking. She said, "My friend, Warren Allen, was with me. Something is terribly wrong around here." She bit her lip. "We couldn't get inside the fort. We were prowling around, seeking an entrance. You see, I have an uncle who is connected with the army. He's supposed to be here at the fort, and I've simply *got* to find him!"

She stopped for breath—or to get her story straight; it was hard to tell which.

"Yes?" Ham prompted.

"Well, that's when everything occurred at once."

"What happened?"

"Warren Allen and I were walking along the base of this wall, and suddenly two men appeared and grabbed him. There was a fight." She paused and shuddered. "Warren gasped out for me to run. I guess that I . . . I got panicky and screamed." Annabel Lynn clutched at Ham's arm again. "And then you appeared . . . and now—we've got to find Warren!"

Monk looked hopeful. If there was going to be a fight, he would enjoy it; the prospects seemed very good.

"Where did they take him?" the chemist demanded.

Annabel Lynn waved her slender arm, and her large gray-blue eyes again mirrored fright.

"Back there some place!" she gasped. "Please hurry!"

They rushed in the direction the girl indicated, but found no Warren Allen—they encountered nothing whatsoever, in fact.

Then they located a huge hole in the fort walls; an aperture where it appeared as though a giant grinding-machine had pulverized sand, rock and stone. The debris which had been the solid wall was a loose heap on the earth.

The hole yawned black and massive before their eyes. Behind it was a wide-open entrance to the fort itself.

"Oh! What did that?" gasped Annabel Lynn.

Ham said in awe, "It looks just like that Treasury Building collapse."

Annabel Lynn's expression was changing; something crept into the depths of her lovely eyes; her shapely hands clenched, and she started trembling. She said in a strange voice, "It— Then it's all true!"

Curious, watching her, Ham asked, "What's true?"

For a moment, it seemed that Annabel Lynn was going to give a reply that made sense. Then her eyes took on a secretive look and she seemed to be fighting to repress and get control of herself.

Monk, puzzled, said, "Well, go on. Tell us. What is the truth? What is behind this?"

Abruptly, the girl's trembling subsided. She looked suddenly composed. "I— It's nothing. It was just something that— I was nervous, and said something that didn't make sense."

"None of it makes sense!" Monk complained.

The girl looked at the hole in the wall and suggested: "We've got to find Warren Allen. Maybe if we crawled through there, we could hear the two men who seized him. They must be carrying Warren."

They followed the girl, but not before they had exchanged significant nudges in the darkness. Perhaps both were recalling that they had seen Annabel Lynn loitering near the scene of that Treasury Building collapse in Washington.

There were things about Annabel Lynn that were puzzling, to say the least.

They found two dead guards inside the fort walls.

Chapter XII

DEATH FOR TWO

The hole in the outer wall was really a tunnel-size opening into a basement storage room of some sort inside the fort. The dead men—they had died in peculiar positions, clutching at their chests—were obviously military watchmen, for they carried watchmen's clocks and apparently had been making the rounds of the huge, grim building. The nature of the fate that had stricken them, dropping them in their tracks, was a mystery. There were no marks on their bodies.

The room itself was a shambles. Various gun parts must have been in neat racks and steel bins along the stone walls; now everything—parts, racks, bits of steel—were scrap iron strewn about the floor.

One wall showed indications of caving in shortly. There were cracks in the thick cement floor.

Annabel Lynn was shaking again.

Ham said quickly, "This place looks none too safe. We'd better get out."

The dapper lawyer produced a flashlight which furnished a white funnel of illumination.

They advanced through various other basementlike rooms, coming finally to a heavy steel door with a sign in red which warned:

KEEP OUT!

Monk, always inquisitive, opened the door, poked in the beam of the flashlight which he had taken from Ham. He howled, "*Yeo-o-ow!*" He jumped back.

The girl and Ham leaped forward to see what had drawn the startled exclamation. Both gasped.

The room was a storage vault for big shells and various kinds of ammunition. There was a conveyer device which led somewhere above, and apparently the shells and other supplies could be quickly moved to gun placements at various points of the fort.

Monk squealed, "Imagine if that . . . that *thing* had hit this place instead of the wall! It would've blown Staten Island over around the State of Iowa somewhere!"

Ham was thoughtful. "I wish Doc was here."

Annabel Lynn's pretty eyes were wide. "I've got to tell Doc Savage the truth," she said grimly. "Only such a man can stop this infernal thing in time."

Ham's eyes went sharp. "Just what do you know about this mystery?" he demanded.

The tall, blond girl frowned at the nattily attired lawyer. "Have you ever been to Rockaway Beach?" she asked unexpectedly.

"No. But I know where it is."

"Well, I was not sure until I trailed it there," the girl said. "I was swimming—when I thought no one was watching—and that terrible shaking sensation seized me. It was like something tearing me apart."

"What was it?"

The girl shuddered. "I know by this time that I miraculously escaped death. Because Rockaway Beach is close to Fort Atlantic, and that is where the gun base collapsed. Uncle Jason knows about that, and he can stop it. I mean, this terrible thing—this whole mess—he can stop it. I've got to find him."

Ham nodded. "Which makes it *all* very clear. I must say," he suggested dryly. "Now listen, why don't you start at the first and tell—"

From behind where they were standing, a harsh voice rapped, "You'd better skip it, sister!"

Monk whirled and let out a gulp. The thick, solid-looking man standing in the opening to a nearby passageway apparently had no gun, although he looked tough enough to get by without one.

The hairy chemist had made a dive for the big fellow. Monk was impulsive. And it was then that the man tossed the egg.

The object landed near Monk's feet, and it made a soft *plop!* Only it wasn't an egg; something that looked like gas and smelled like a boiled cabbage spread through the passageway.

Ham and Monk and the girl also jumped clear of the gas mushrooming from the hard floor.

The big, thickset attacker had dived back into an adjoining room. Monk rushed after him, howling at the same time—those fighting howls of Monk's were extraordinary; usually Monk talked in a thin, piping voice, but once he got in battle, he bellowed like a bull.

Monk made a flying tackle at the big man's legs, dragged the fellow to the floor. Then Monk picked up the assailant, and bounced him off the nearest wall. Ham, unsheathing his sword-cane, had moved in to help. But the hairy chemist's heave had knocked the attacker senseless.

Monk figured that he was getting started at making a favorable impression on attractive Annabel Lynn. "I could lick a half dozen like him," Monk boasted.

He got his chance. Three more men came piling out of a doorway and rushed to the attack. Monk whooped. Ham swung to meet the attack with his sword-cane.

Annabel Lynn seized Ham's flashlight and sprayed light over the scene.

A gun went off, its crash resounding around the stone walls. Ham's sword caught the man's gun arm, knocked it upward, and bullets dug dust and cement from the ceiling. One of the attackers screamed a warning against using guns. "You fool!" the assailant screeched at his companion. "Stop shooting! The shock may set off some of this stored ammunition!"

Thereafter the fight settled into a catch-as-catch-can, knock-down-and-drag-out mêlée. Monk yelled and banged heads together. Ham, with deft movements of his sword, herded the attackers Monk's way for the chemist to put on the finishing touches.

Then the attackers began leaving the room as though it were full of rattlesnakes. They had enough. They went clattering and panting down a long passageway. They passed through a door and slammed it, made it fast.

The door was very strong; it took time for Monk and Ham to tear it down—time enough for their defeated assailants to escape, for they found no trace of the men.

It was Annabel Lynn who exclaimed worriedly, "The—whoever is behind this menace—is getting frantic! They'll kill all of us—including Doc Savage!"

Monk said, "Not if they don't do better than they've been doing."

Ham decided it might be a good idea if they went back and questioned the big man Monk had knocked out. Returning, they found that the gas had cleared the space. And so had the big fellow. He had disappeared.

"Boy, I'll hit the next one so hard he won't wake up that quick!" Monk said.

Ham suggested, "We might search farther."

Later, they located a stairway that led upward.

Ham was carrying the flashlight in one hand, his sword-cane in the other. Annabel Lynn clung to Monk's arm, causing the hairy chemist to grin at Ham.

They passed through huge, vault-like rooms, emerged finally upon a drill grounds; beyond were dark, sinister gun pits of the long-range guns. They saw no one, heard no one.

"Queer this place is so deserted," Monk said.

Ham said quietly, "I remember reading that this place was temporarily closed."

Annabel, trembling, said wildly, "Mercy, if anything happens to Uncle Jason or . . . or Warren Allen! I . . . I understood that Uncle Jason could be found here."

"What made you think Uncle Jason would be here?"

"A . . . a note he sent me."

"Just who is this Uncle Jason?"

Annabel did not answer the question directly, but explained, "You see, the fort is temporarily closed. Those dead watchmen back there were probably the only men on duty. But in a few days coast artillery units are scheduled to arrive here for new-gun practice. Uncle Jason was to be here, to meet someone from Washington tonight. They were making some . . . some kind of preliminary plans, I think. I . . . I don't know much about Uncle Jason's relations with the army."

Just then, through the gloom of the outside drill yard, they heard someone walking.

Ham unsheathed his sword-cane, and sturdy Monk stood ready to jump whoever was approaching. Ham also snapped off his light.

Monk muttered, "Watch me pop this guy one!"

The steps, quick with haste, came closer. Ham said, "All right—now!" and switched on the light.

Annabel Lynn cried, "Warren!"

Both aids of Doc Savage stared. In the flashlight glare was revealed the perfectly attired young Englishman of the Washington restaurant—Warren Allen.

"They escaped from me!" Warren Allen explained.

Chapter XIII

PERSONS MISSING

Warren Allen's expensive imported clothes were mussed. His light-blond hair had been rumpled.

"That attack on you, Warren? What happened?" Annabel asked.

Apparently the man had remarkable emotional control, for he seemed unaffected by the incident. Calmly, he said, "I broke loose from them, escaped, and later trailed them down to the beach. They left in a small boat, because I heard a gas engine out there on the water." He hesitated, then shrugged. "I wasn't too keen on tangling with them. They were armed."

"Do *you* know what is behind all this mystery?" Ham demanded.

"No idea at all."

"But you're mixed up in it."

"I am only helping Annabel Lynn," Warren Allen explained virtuously. "She asked me to come with her to help find her uncle. It was a night trip, and this is a lonely spot for a girl alone, so naturally I came."

Ham suggested, "We've got to find a phone and get in touch with Doc. He will want to know about this trouble here."

He led the way back into the fort. Apparently lights in the place had been put out of commission by the force that had smashed a gigantic hole through one wall, for Ham tried several light switches and got no results. He continued to use his flashlight. The others trailed behind the lunging beam of light.

"Let's scatter and look for a phone," Ham said. They separated.

In a small room, evidently a commander's office, Ham found a desk phone. He lifted the receiver and rattled the hook. For a while, he waited patiently. There was no answer.

Impatient, the lawyer rattled the hook and said, "Operator! Operator!" with some sharpness.

The line was dead, and Ham turned with the idea of rejoining Monk, Warren Allen and the girl, who could not be far away.

A man appeared in the doorway with a great deal of blue-steel gun in his fist and snarled, "That phone ain't all that's gonna be out of order around here!" The man stepped into the room, gun leveling.

Ham jumped, snapping off his flash and yanking his slender sword-cane from its polished, wooden sheath. The tip of the blade was coated with quick-acting anaesthetic, and it frequently saved the lawyer's life.

Ham moved smoothly, in total darkness, instinct telling him about where the other man was. Abruptly, the gun made a loud sound in the small room; it almost hurt Ham's eardrums.

Luckily, the lead went wild. Ham stepped forward, speared with the sword. He sought what he hoped was his attacker's chest.

Ham, however, made an error—he got too close to the man. Something came out of the gloom and connected with his lean jaw. He had a hunch what it was—one of the long ramrodlike cleaning bars for the big guns. It took the lawyer off his feet, threw him across the room and piled him headfirst into the far wall.

As he passed out, he had a hazy recollection of someone

snapping, "Now we better get the one that looks like an apel"

Monk was having troubles of his own at the moment. As he had ambled into a room looking for a telephone, something had hit him solidly from behind.

A muffled scream from the girl, Annabel Lynn, and the beginning of an outcry from Warren Allen made the disaster rather complete.

Monk, dazed but far from kayoed, went into action. They were trying—more than one man had hold of him—to half drag, half shove him into some space that was beyond the room where Ham had disappeared. It seemed to Monk that a dozen thugs must have jumped him.

Fists slugged away at his battered jaw; knuckles raked his scarred features. It didn't take much of that to get Monk mad. He grabbed assorted legs, arms, heads and did all the battering he could. He heard breath explode from tortured lungs; yelps of pain come from his unseen assailants' throats.

Monk convulsed and threw off his attackers as though they were so many midgets. He bellowed, and cracked heads together. After a while he drew up short, and he realized that he was swinging at air.

"Blazes!" he snorted, disappointed. He stumbled over senseless figures, bent down, searched through pockets until he found a flashlight. Switching it on, he took one look at the unconscious forms, shrugged and dashed out to see what had happened to the girl and her friend. Also what had detained his partner Ham.

And Monk found no one. No Ham. No girl. No Warren Allen.

Monk started a more complete search of the place.

Ten minutes later, worried and puzzled about the disappearance of everyone, Monk raced to the car which he and Ham had driven to the fort. Perhaps they had gone back to the machine.

But they hadn't. There was no one at the car.

Monk decided he had better reach Doc. Climbing in the car, he switched on the short-wave radio transmitter receiver located behind the dash. When the set warmed up, he tried to raise a reply from Doc's skyscraper headquarters.

He did not get Doc—what he got, instead, was a dull rumbling noise that mystified him at first; then he realized that it was a voice, Renny's voice, and the giant engineer was saying over and over:

"Doc, are you listening in? Long Tom and I seized somewhere near Connecticut shore. Probably near New London. Doc, hope you are listening in. Long Tom and I need help. Hurry!"

Renny's bull-like voice soon faded. Monk whirled various knobs on the special built-in set. All he could get was hum of the tubes themselves and static.

"Hell's bells!" yelled Monk, who rarely used profanity.

He forgot the senseless men back at the fort. He forgot everything but getting in touch with Doc Savage as soon as possible.

Monk sent the big car hurtling toward New York. In a remarkably short time, he was in the express elevator being lifted to the bronze man's headquarters. The sun was rising over the horizon and shining brightly through hallway windows up here high above the still-dozing city.

Monk, his short, stocky legs moving like pistons, hurried to the great door of bronze that was the main entrance to the skyscraper headquarters.

The door opened before the chemist was barely up to it, and Monk started to exclaim, "Doc—"

But it wasn't Doc.

It was homely Nanny Hanks, and she let out a cry of joy, jumped toward the chemist with open arms and said, "You poor dear! Look at your face and clothes! Something terrible must have happened to you!"

Monk backed off from the woman and stood glaring. Finally, he blurted, "Look, Ham is missing!"

"Yes, but—"

"Annabel is missing!"

Nanny Hanks grimaced.

"And Warren Allen is missing! And now Long Tom and Renny are in some kind of jam. Have I got trouble!"

"You poor dear!" said Nanny Hanks solicitously.

Monk threw up his arms, dropped wearily into a chair. "And now *you* turn up!" He shook his head sadly, asked, "How did you get in?"

"I guess the place wasn't locked. I walked in."

"You started out with us—and we missed you down in front of the building. What happened?"

"I went in a drugstore to get some aspirin. This thing is giving me a headache. When I came out, you were gone. You ran off and left me." Nanny Hanks looked sadly at Monk and asked, "You said Renny and Long Tom are in trouble?"

Monk nodded dismally. "Yep."

"Well, I can tell you something about them."

Monk jumped. "What?"

"I picked them up on the short-wave radio here," Nanny Hanks went on. "They discovered something out there at Fort Atlantic, on Long Island."

"Yes?"

"And now they've been grabbed by somebody, because of what they found out."

That seemed to be all that Nanny Hanks knew about the two aids of Doc Savage, Monk discovered. He wondered how Nanny Hanks happened to be a radio operator—the short-wave set up here was complicated. For that matter, there were a number of things about Nanny Hanks that made food for wondering, once one started thinking.

Chapter XIV

TRUCK THAT DISAPPEARED

Nanny Hanks had been correct in stating that Long Tom and big-fisted Renny were in trouble; she had not been trying to fool Monk on that point. But she was in error on one thing—the giant engineer and his sickly-looking partner were now nowhere near Fort Atlantic; they were captives in a plane somewhere over Connecticut.

True, they had been at Fort Atlantic. Following Doc's instructions, Renny and Long Tom had proceeded to the Long Island fort in one of the bronze man's planes. There, they had spent considerable time making an investigation questioning officers, building-engineers and contractors.

But no one had any explanation for a gun foundation that pulverized into loose sand and crumpled cement.

It was some time after this that Long Tom, prowling through the disintegrated foundation with a flashlight, suddenly scooped up a fistful of sand and examined it closely.

Long Tom exclaimed after a moment, "Might pay us to analyze this!"

Renny, watching his unhealthy-looking partner, remarked, "Holy cow! It's only plain sand. What can you learn from that?"

"What's the harm in trying?" asked Long Tom.

They saw fort officials, and were given permission to use a small but well-equipped laboratory on the reservation. Long Tom was an electrical wizard; he had often been compared with that electrical genius the late Steinmetz. Though sand and cement particles appeared to be a peculiar thing to interest an electrical expert, they nevertheless held Long Tom's attention.

Long Tom, watched by Renny, finally straightened from the laboratory workbench and exclaimed, "I think I've got something here!"

It was near dawn; the two aids were alone in the small laboratory. The remainder of the army reservation was in darkness.

Big Renny's voice boomed in the small room. "Got what?"

"The reason for that gun-base foundation disintegrating," continued Long Tom. "Also, something else." Long Tom's eyes were very bright in his pale face. His mop of pale hair was rumpled, almost standing on end.

"Well, what? Holy cow! Cut out the suspense."

"I can tell you what is doing it!" Long Tom almost shouted.

At this point, there was a discreet knock on the door of the small lab, and Renny turned to answer it, opening the door. A nattily uniformed sergeant stood outside, a man who said quietly, "Sorry to disturb you gentlemen. But the commander wishes to see you."

"Commander?"

"Yes. It's quite important. I have a car waiting."

A moment later Renny and Long Tom followed the army sergeant outside. Long Tom stared about in the night. He exclaimed, "What the hell! I don't see any car!"

A dozen more men appeared out of the darkness. They hardly had the military appearance of trained soldiers. They were a dozen assorted thugs in khaki—not even wearing regulation army fatigue garb, but merely garments which resembled regulation.

They closed in on Renny and Long Tom, and short clubs the dozen men carried started swinging at the two

Doc aids. Someone growled in Long Tom's thin face, "Brother, I reckon you figured out this business too late!"

The assailants made an error in sizing up skinny Long Tom and Renny. They had evidently decided that the giant engineer, Renny, might give them trouble, but puny-looking Long Tom would be a cinch. One man only tackled the thin electrical wizard; the rest made for Renny.

The one man found himself flat on the ground within a second after he made a clutch for Long Tom.

The other men were piling on giant Renny. Long Tom flew into the mêlée and started grabbing throats, and the attackers conceivably got the impression a bobcat had suddenly been turned loose. Long Tom moved with blurred, amazing speed.

Renny was flailing with his two pail-size fists.

The fight—a tangled, swaying, snarling mass—worked its way toward the nearby beach. Purposefully, Renny and Long Tom got the mêlée into the surf. They ducked heads into the salty water.

More attackers came running along the beach, to the aid of their henchmen. That finished the affair. Renny and Long Tom were overpowered, knocked senseless.

They were carried to their own plane and dumped into the baggage compartment. They were then tied hand and foot. The plane, carrying Renny and Long Tom and some of their captors, then took off in the darkness preceding dawn.

It was some time later that Renny, recovering from the knockout, managed to squirm his way along the floor of the baggage compartment in which they had been locked, and managed to locate a spare short-wave radio. The radio was an emergency unit carried in one of Doc's metal equipment cases. Renny got it out, put it in operation, and began calling with his mouth so close to the mike that his tone was a mumble.

From conversation overheard by Renny, he estimated their whereabouts. Feet and hands bound, and his thoughts rather hazy, he did his best.

This was the call that Monk had heard on Staten Island, and which had sent him back to headquarters—the same call of which Nanny Hanks told Monk at Doc Savage's headquarters.

Back at Doc Savage's headquarters, Nanny Hanks and homely Monk were puzzled—or at least, Monk was bewildered. They had not decided what should be done. Monk, also, was no little worried about the predicament of his partner Ham.

Shortly after this, Ham arrived—not the smartly dressed, dapper pride of Harvard, but a bedraggled, weary-looking Ham, with his face bruised, his expensively tailored clothes in shreds. Even his usually polished sword-cane was scuffed.

Ham stalked into the room and sank into a chair.

"Where's Annabel Lynn?" Monk asked.

"Haven't you got her?" Ham demanded. "There was a lot of excitement out at that fort, and when it was over, I couldn't find anybody. I just got back from there."

"No, I haven't got the girl. I thought she was with you."

"That's a fine note!" Ham complained. He lifted his voice to a yell. "Why in blazes didn't you take care of her, you homely dope!"

Nanny Hanks got between the two aids before mayhem could be committed.

She said, "Mercy me, you two better think about Doc Savage!"

"Doc?" Ham asked. "What's wrong?"

"He left a message for you," said Nanny Hanks quietly.

Monk jumped. "Message?"

It was the first time Nanny Hanks had mentioned the message.

"I heard it," said the stout woman, matter-of-factly. She motioned to a cabinet built into the wall. "It's on that recording machine."

The machine was a device constructed with two electromagnets, between which passed a thin steel wire. The apparatus used a similar principle to the phonograph, only in this case the recording was made by variable magnetizing of the wire instead of on a record. By playing the wire back, the original recording could be obtained.

Ham ran the wire through the instrument and the deep, magnetic voice of Doc Savage said, "Have gone to Connecticut. Renny and Long Tom in trouble near New London. Suspect they are held at some cove near there. And whole mystery seems to have that direction. Let Nanny Hanks help you and follow. Will contact you later."

Monk groaned. "I heard Renny callin' for help, too! Got the message just before I drove back here from the fort." The chemist suddenly looked worried, added: "Blazes, what about Annabel Lynn and that Englishman? You say you never saw them after we got separated, lookin' for a telephone there at the fort?"

Ham shrugged hopelessly. "They were gone. No trace of them. I have a hunch those crooks captured them and made off in a boat."

For a moment, there was gloomy silence.

Ham growled something and started toward another room, to get a change of clothing.

Nanny Hanks said, "Wait, you two. You want to know something?"

Monk would have liked to ignore the woman, but curiosity impelled him to ask, "What?"

"I know where that Long Tom and Renny are!"

Both men gave a start. Ham had paused in the doorway to the adjoining room. His eyes narrowed, and he said, "You seem to know everything. How come you're so full of information, but you only put it out by dabs and dribbles?"

Monk scowled and added, "Yeah. How come?"

"Don't you ever trust anybody when they ask you to?" Nanny Hanks countered.

"Not if I can get out of it."

"I don't see how you can get out of trusting me," Nanny Hanks said. "I know where Renny and Long Tom probably can be found. I'll take you there. Or you can refuse my help, if you wish."

"We're not refusing anybody's help," Monk said.

Shortly after this, they got started. They went back down to the street, where Monk had left the limousine; Nanny Hanks and Ham piled in.

They failed to notice the truck which pulled away from the curb a half block behind them. The vehicle was one similar to the sound trucks used by news-reel companies, only its paneled sides were painted black. The truck kept behind the two aids of Doc Savage as they drove toward Connecticut.

Doc Savage was flying low over the curving Connecticut shore line. The bronze man, using binoculars occasionally, was at the moment intent on scanning every inlet and cove that was tucked away south of New London. The plane in which Doc flew was the government ship borrowed at the time of Doc's experience with Philips, the would-be killer who had been slain before he could give information while under the influence of truth serum.

The fact that the bronze man had borrowed a military plane was being kept secret. Now that Doc Savage's life was in danger, there was no sense of inviting menace by taking the chances of enemies recognizing one of his own planes. Government planes of this type were plentiful enough to confuse a foe.

The mystery had cropped up in a new place. During the night, so Doc had been informed, a submarine lying at anchor at the New London sub base, had gone to the bottom. Luckily, no men had been lost. Divers had been sent down to learn what had caused the sinking of the sub.

Their report had been that a section of the submarine had collapsed. It could have hardly been a flaw in the workmanship, for the sub had been in commission for some months. As one diver reported, it was as though some impossible force had caused a good portion of the sub to simply collapse.

Furthermore, Doc had picked up Renny's call for aid. That had simplified matters a great deal, for Renny had left the portable radio which he had used switched on, and it had been a simple matter to use the direction finder with which the navy plane was equipped. Doc had been rotating the directional loop, watching the pointer, comparing it with the compass card—and flying, he knew, steadily nearer and nearer the radio which Renny had used.

Suddenly, as the bronze man leaned over the cockpit and studied the shore line below, he dipped his elevators and dropped swiftly. His flake-gold eyes were sharp.

To any other observer, the cove which Doc had just passed might have appeared as a sleepy, deserted little inlet far out near an isolated, drab bit of coast line. Trees grew up close to the water's edge; there wasn't a sign of life anywhere.

But concealed beneath tree branches dipping over the shore edge, Doc Savage saw the bit of something that gleamed in the hot sun. He circled low, came back, throttled his motors, and skimmed more closely over the quiet-looking inlet. This time his unusual eyes caught sight of a low metal wing, streamlined and sleek—the wing of a fast amphibian plane moored close under the trees along the shore, and covered with fresh-cut branches.

There was nothing unusual about a plane being tied up in a cove along a bit of lonesome Connecticut coast—but what was startling was that the plane was one of the bronze man's own ships! The radio he had traced down with the direction finder was obviously on that ship.

Doc Savage barely grazed the treetops with the plane's undercarriage, gunned the motor, gained a little altitude and took a quick survey of the shore line beneath him. Adjacent to the cove in which he had seen his own ship, he saw another inlet that was one of the many indentations in this dreary stretch of land.

He glided down to a smooth landing, taxied toward the shore, cut his motors and climbed out in hip-deep water. The inlet was calm, smooth. He anchored the navy plane and started quickly toward the nearby woods that crowded close to a rocky beach.

Doc considered the possible fate that might have befallen Renny and Long Tom as he worked his way silently toward the adjacent cove. The big engineer and the electrical wizard, Long Tom, had been sent to the Long Island location of Fort Atlantic to investigate the mystery of the worthless gun-base. The two aids had used one of Doc's amphibians for a quick flight to the fort—which was the last he had heard of them until now a call for aid had come over the special wave length used by all the bronze man's radio sets. Obviously, it had come from the streamlined amphibian lying here in this cove. So Renny and Long Tom had been in trouble on their own plane.

He kept to the woods, circled the cove until he was beyond and behind the concealed plane. Doc heard no movement. It was hot and quiet. Bees buzzed lazily somewhere close by; evidently there was a bee tree near.

For several moments, from concealing bushes, Doc watched the moored plane. Apparently there was no one about. Silently, he moved out into the open and headed quickly toward the ship. It was only necessary to take a dozen steps through shallow water in order to reach the amphibian; he swung agilely aboard.

There was a control compartment forward, a small cabin to the rear of this. Doc opened the cabin door, squinted his eyes a trifle against the gloom inside the ship, then stepped inside. Muffled through-the-nose sounds came from the two figures lying bound and gagged upon the floor.

One figure was well over six feet, with a long sad face that looked as unhappy as an undertaker viewing the Fountain of Eternal Youth, and who, when untied, stood up and said, "Holy cow, Doc!" in a voice that crashed in the cabin interior.

"You hurt, Renny?" Doc asked.

"My dignity hasn't been helped any."

"How about Long Tom?"

"Oh, they didn't do anything but boot both of us around," Renny said. "However, I think they were going to kill us later."

Doc got Long Tom untied and on his feet.

"You two might explain what happened."

Renny rumbled, "We got out to Fort Atlantic. Long Tom discovered something about the way the cement of that antiaircraft gun base had disintegrated, and was just going to report the fact when an army of guys jumped us."

"At least a dozen of them," Long Tom put in more accurately. "They got us tied up and took us to our plane. And here we are!"

"Where are the men now?"

"They're somewhere close, I think. We gathered that they only kept us alive because they're meeting someone near here. Seems they're waiting for some further orders. Incidentally, while we were flying here, Renny managed to crawl to the microphone and send out that message before they came back to gag him."

"You have any ideas about this thing?" Doc asked the electrical wizard.

"It's something which is moving from place to place." Long Tom frowned. "But I can't understand why it has got a mad on at government buildings. Hell, we ain't at war with anybody!"

"That's true," admitted the bronze man. "And yet, whatever this thing is, it is obviously directing itself against the security of coast-line fortifications."

Renny, puzzled, asked, "Anybody declared war on us."

Doc shook his head. "Relations with all foreign countries are the same as usual," he said.

"Which means everybody in Europe's tryin' to borrow money from us," boomed Renny.

Doc, happening to glance outside the cabin window, said quietly, "It wouldn't be surprising if those men yonder were some of them."

His two aids swung to follow Doc's gaze, and it was big Renny who breathed, "Holy cow! Look at the size of them. If you ask me, every one of those guys is a trained soldier."

At least a dozen men of massive stature were lined along the shore. Several had already started through the shallow water toward the plane. Nordic in type, all well over six feet, the men spoke to each other in a foreign tongue.

They had no suspicion of trouble.

When they were very near the plane, Doc Savage moved. The cabin door had been open. From the pocket of his concealed equipment vest. Doc grasped a fistful of small pellets. Several of these he tossed out upon the water, in front of the approaching mob.

Immediately, the water must have created some chemical reaction in the pellets, for they burst with terrific detonations, knocked up sheets of water, and blue flame seared the nearer of the yelling attackers. They started to retreat with singed faces and scorched hair.

"Come on!" Renny bellowed. He leaped out of the plane, followed by unhealthy-looking Long Tom. Doc threw some more of the pellets and joined his two aids.

The exploding missiles created a barrage behind which moved Doc and his partners. Renny leaped through a sheet of rising flame, let out a bull roar and started swinging.

Within seconds, everyone of the blond-haired giants had disappeared into the woods. The surprise had been complete.

For a while there was yelling and the sound of brush being trampled and confusion. And finally—silence. Silence that was thick and still and enveloping.

"They're gone," Doc advised. "We might remove the distributor mechanism from the motor so that they cannot steal the ship in case they do come back. Also, try contacting Monk and Ham. A woman named Nanny Hanks is with them."

Doc Savage explained briefly about the woman undercover operative. He said nothing regarding her forged identification card—strangely enough, the bronze man seemed content to give Nanny Hanks free rein.

Long Tom removed an essential part from the distributor on the motor; the motor could not possibly be started without the part. Next, he moved into the cockpit, and tuned in the short-wave radio. Tubes hummed. "Hello Monk—hello Ham," Long Tom said into the microphone.

"Blazes!" said a small voice from the speaker.

"That's Monk!" Long Tom exclaimed. Doc and Renny had joined him.

Doc picked up the microphone. "Monk?" he queried.

The hairy chemist yelled, "Doc, where are you? Have you found Renny and Long Tom?"

Doc explained what had taken place, gave his location, asked where the chemist and his partner were now.

Monk replied, "U. S. Highway ten miles west of New London. Look, Doc, there's been a truck following us all morning. We're lettin' them keep us in sight, and thought we might lead them into a trap."

"What kind of truck?" Doc asked.

"One of the movie sound trucks, it looks like," Monk hurried.

Doc's eyes were suddenly thoughtful.

He said quickly, "Keep the truck in sight, Monk. And now here's what you are to do."

The bronze man, in coming down for a landing on the adjacent inlet, had taken in the surrounding terrain carefully. The U. S. highway ten miles west of New London passed through a village only about two or three miles from this isolated shore spot, and Doc had observed a dusty, winding road that led from the main highway back in this direction.

Doc gave brief directions, told the hairy chemist how close they could come to this inlet by taking the old road. He finished with, "Let those in the truck see you turn in here. Draw them in. That is important. We'll handle the rest."

"O. K., Doc," said Monk.

Later, Doc and Long Tom and Renny waited somewhere along the narrow dusty road, where it wound down and ended in woods near the shore. The big limousine containing Monk and Ham, and Nanny Hanks swung into view.

Doc quickly directed the car beneath concealing trees off the road.

"Where's the trailing truck?"

"Close behind us!" Monk explained.

Sending Nanny Hanks to a place of safety, Doc and his men prepared to waylay the truck. They waited five minutes . . . ten.

It was obvious that their quarry had, either through luck or cleverness, outsmarted them.

Chapter XV

DOC TRAILS NANNY

At ten that same night, the disappearance of the sound truck, the vanishing of tall and regal Annabel Lynn and her friend, Warren Allen, remained a puzzle.

Monk and Ham, worried about Annabel, had told Doc Savage what they knew of Uncle Jason, whom the blond girl was seeking. Apparently, Jason was the key to the mystery, Monk and Ham assured Doc that the girl had told them.

Search for the sound truck had covered nearby Connecticut communities, but they had found no trace of the vehicle.

At ten thirty, Doc Savage contacted an army official in New York, using a radio set installed in the army plane that had been placed at his disposal. Doc spoke for some time with the official.

He came back to report, "Annabel Lynn and Warren Allen are somewhere near New London. They have been seen there tonight."

When they joined homely Nanny Hanks, she made no

comment as Annabel Lynn's name was mentioned. Previously, she'd always had a remark to put in. But since the bronze man's statement concerning Annabel Lynn and Warren Allen being seen somewhere near New London, Nanny Hanks had remained unusually quiet.

It was shortly after this that Monk, looking around to make certain that Nanny Hanks wasn't on the verge of making another pass at him, let out a startled bark.

"What's wrong with you now?" Ham asked.

"She's gone again!"

"Who?"

"That vanishing wonder around here—Nanny Hanks!"

Doc Savage seemed to reach an abrupt decision; he spoke tersely.

"All of you start a search for Annabel Lynn and that friend of hers—the Englishman," Doc ordered. "Bring them back here, if you locate them."

Without further explanations, Doc left his men. The bronze man—he had not mentioned the fact to the others—had seen the departure of Nanny Hanks; he had watched, and he knew in what direction she had gone. He now followed her through the night.

The bronze giant carried a small case taken from the limousine that Monk and Ham had driven out from New York—a metal case of the type used as containers for the variety of scientific gadgets which he had occasion to use.

Nanny Hanks lost no time in reaching the main highway that led toward the seaport town of New London. She got out on the highway pavement and started trying to thumb a ride; there was determination in the way she went about getting a lift.

Doc Savage, suspecting her purpose, moved back to the security of high bushes bordering the road. In the next few moments, as Nanny Hanks tried for rides, the bronze man worked quickly with materials taken from the equipment case.

When the woman undercover operative was picked up by a passing truck, a bent, long-looking farmer appeared beside the road and raced after the vehicle. The stoop-shouldered farmer was Doc Savage, and he managed to swing onto the tailboard of the truck. The highway was a through route to Boston; many trucks were on the road, and there was considerable traffic noise, so that it was very infrequently that Doc caught a word from the driver's compartment.

Seated in the big cab of the truck, the driver asked, "Going far, mom?"

"Reckon not," she said. "Just a piece. I'll let you know after a bit where I want to git out."

Doc, moving back to the rear of the truck, watched the road and wondered if the woman's destination was New London.

They were soon entering the street-lighted outskirts of the town. Rumbling through downtown streets, Doc kept a sharp lookout, prepared for the truck to stop. It did not halt.

They rolled on out of town, across the narrow Thames River, then the truck suddenly slowed. Doc dropped off quickly, took cover and watched Nanny Hanks climb out. The section was a river-front district of shacks and places to hire fishing boats and tackle.

The bronze man waited until the truck had gone on, and Nanny Hanks had moved ahead, then stepped out boldly and followed the homely woman, depending on his disguise.

Soon he was walking back along the side of the highway, thence down a flight of rickety wooden steps that led to a string of fishing shacks and water-front boat-rental docks.

Being summer, and warm, many of the places were open all night. They rented canoes, rowboats and skiffs for fishing. Several buildings ahead, Doc saw dumpy Nanny Hanks climbing into a flat-bottomed rowboat; evidently she had just rented the craft.

Doc, stalling for time, started looking over some boats. Perhaps a farmer interested in taking himself a night rowboat ride was a little unusual, but when Doc tendered a sizable deposit to the caretaker on duty, no questions were asked.

Nanny Hanks had disappeared downstream, rowing close along the shore, by the time Doc pushed off in his own craft. A significant point occurred to the bronze man. On this very side of the Thames, not far above here, was located the U. S. Naval Station and submarine base. But Nanny Hanks apparently was not headed that way—she was going downriver toward Long Island Sound, less than three miles away. Doc followed quietly, making no noise as he managed the oars expertly in the calm water.

After a while, Doc heard no dip of oars ahead, no creak of oarlocks in the still night. He held his own oars out of the water and listened tensely.

Ahead, a voice spoke challengingly. Nanny Hanks replied. Then the two voices lowered, and there was talking; Doc could not catch the words. But he heard the woman's rowboat bump some kind of dock; then steps were hurrying swiftly along a stringpiece. There was a sharp clank like an iron door closing and then silence.

Doc moved ahead quietly, found a wooden dock, carefully tied his rowboat. He swung up a ladder to the planks, started walking toward shore, then halted.

On the far side of the dock something loomed up out of the water—something that hardly belonged here, several miles downriver from the naval station. It was the conning tower of a small submarine, and the major part of the sub was beneath water level.

With as little sound as possible, Doc stepped down a short gangplank that led to the conning tower hatchway. His powerful fingers, working carefully, found and gripped the hatch opening and raised silently.

A glow of light came from the control room below, and voices talking, several of them. Doc listened.

Nanny Hanks was saying. "—and so he'll be at the navy yard tomorrow. You can make an appointment with him."

"At what time?" a voice with a foreign accent asked.

"About eleven o'clock tomorrow morning," replied Nanny Hanks.

"Jason Lynn is ready to make a deal, yes?" The speaker had a sleekly smooth voice, markedly foreign.

"Yes," said Nanny Hanks briefly. "I understand you are moving to the base near Boston tonight."

"Correct."

"And what about this girl—this Annabel Lynn?"

The purring laugh came again. "Don't worry about Annabel Lynn!"

That seemed to be the end of the interview; there was sound of feet moving about. Doc started to lower the hatch opening—and someone landed on his back with the force of a hurtling juggernaut.

He was thrown to one side by the impact. The hatch cover slipped from his grasp, slapped down with a crash. Doc whirled, tried to reach for the shoulders of the man who had somehow managed to slip up on him so silently.

He saw three figures. Vague, heavy men, menacing forms in the gloom of the river front. The one man who had jumped the bronze man gripped Doc's arms. He yelled to his two assistants, "Quick! Slug him!"

But Doc took them off guard. He moved with blurred speed, sent the man holding his arms over his head. The fellow landed in a sprawl somewhere on the dock. Another assailant leaped in, confident that he was going to finish off the man in the farmer's garb. An arm slapped him sidewise and he tumbled into the water.

The third found hands around his neck; he was yanked off his feet. He went up in the air, kicking frantically, and he did a somersault, hit the water alongside the dock.

Doc Savage had no desire to be recognized; so far, wearing the disguise, he did not believe they had guessed his identity. He deliberately let the first of the men coming up out of the sub hit him with a pipe wrench. He had seen the wrench as the man came out of the hatch; it swung a second later, and Doc let it land, being sure to go backward so that the blow had no more force than a hard-slugging fist.

Doc toppled backward toward the water, made a splash as he hit the surface and went under. He didn't come up.

The wrench-wielder yelled, "Got him! He's done for!"

Men crowded around the string-piece and looked relieved when the slugged figure did not again come to the surface.

"Who was he?"

"Some apple-knocker who came aboard to gander."

"He hear anything?"

"What difference does it make now?"

Doc Savage dived deep, swam underwater for many yards and emerged some distance from the spot, coming up close to shore, then working his way carefully out of the river. On dry land he moved silently through marsh grass bordering the spot.

Sometime after midnight, the bronze man returned to the meeting place at the cove where the amphibian plane was anchored.

His men had not yet returned, so Doc left a message for them.

Then he took his borrowed army plane that was still lying at anchor in the adjacent inlet and flew to New York.

Chapter XVI

JASON

Sometime before dawn that morning, there was mysterious trouble at the defense fortification outside the channel entrance to Boston Harbor. The fort was built on a point of land near Neponset. The single road that wound out to the spot was always under heavy guard; later, army sentries on the road declared no movement of cars or persons had occurred during the night. Likewise, airplane sound-detectors placed at strategic points along the coast line showed no unaccounted-for planes in the vicinity.

But nevertheless a fantastic thing happened at the fortification, and somehow the news leaked out and got into the newspapers. Extras were on the downtown Boston streets by ten o'clock that morning. And Doc Savage read the headlines as he rode toward a Boston hotel.

Several gun placements at Fort Point—that was the newest location menaced—had completely collapsed, apparently by some power that had weirdly disintegrated sand, stone and cement. Huge long-range guns, so the papers said, were useless wrecks embedded in the pulverized foundations. It would take weeks to dig them out, and even then many of the long-range weapons themselves were said to be so damaged as to be worthless.

Less than a half hour before, the bronze man had arrived from New York. He had left the army plane at New York, returned in one of his own planes. A strange assortment of equipment was stored in the plane, where it was under police guard in Boston Harbor. Besides his visit to the Boston hotel—the Pilgrim Prince—Doc was also anxious for word from Renny, Long Tom and the others. On his message left at the meeting place at the cove, he had mentioned this hotel.

The desk clerk nodded, "Colonel Jason Lynn will see you at once, Mr. Savage. Room 213."

Doc got up and disappeared toward the elevators, and as he did so, Monk and Ham, in some kind of heated argument, walked into the hotel entrance.

Neither of them had seen the bronze man, although they had found the message about the meeting at this hotel.

A girl with pretty red hair had paused to glance at dapper Ham, the scarred-faced, homely-looking Monk.

The red-haired girl giggled, then hurried toward the exit of the hotel.

A moment later the page boy came up to Ham and Monk and asked, "Are you the gentlemen who are to meet Mr. Savage?"

They nodded.

"Well, you are to go up to Room 213," said the page boy.

Upstairs, they were introduced to Jason Lynn by Doc Savage.

Jason Lynn was a large, pompous man with heavy walrus mustache and a prominent stomach, rather the picture of a comic-strip financier.

Doc Savage said, "This is Jason Lynn, Annabel's uncle. We had just agreed on that fact when you arrived."

"Yes, I have a niece named Annabel Lynn," agreed the old fellow.

"Then," said Monk, "you can explain this business of

things falling to pieces. Now, start at the beginning and tell us the whole story."

"I don't know what you're talking about," Jason Lynn said.

"You don't!"

"Emphatically."

Monk looked a little groggy. "You mean to tell me that we've got our noses in another empty hole?" The homely chemist turned to Doc Savage. "Maybe this is the wrong Uncle Jason, Doc."

"He is the only Uncle Jason that Annabel Lynn has," Doc explained. "I checked with people who know Annabel Lynn—you will recall that she was fairly well known in Washington—and this is the only Uncle Jason she owns."

"I'm sure Annabel has no other Uncle Jason," said Jason Lynn.

"Perhaps," ventured Jason Lynn, "you are victims of one of my niece's hallucinations."

"Hallucinations?"

"Off moments, if you like that expression better," said Jason Lynn. He assumed an air of reluctantly making an admission. "You see, my niece Annabel does queer things at times. I am afraid—well, she had a hard fall when she was a child, which might explain it."

When Doc Savage was downstairs and out on the street, he moved to a spot where Monk and Ham had parked the large limousine.

Renny and Long Tom were waiting in the machine.

"Any luck?" Long Tom asked.

Monk made a zero circle with his fingers.

"Yes, let's kind of have a roundup," Renny suggested. "It might help."

Ham said, "I'll contribute this much: We know that buildings, planes, forts and guns are falling to pieces."

"Yeah. As if an angry ghost was goin' around raisin' the dickens," Monk said.

"Where do you get that ghost stuff, stupid?" Ham demanded.

Renny boomed, "Ghost, or no ghost, there's men mixed up in it, too. A mysterious gang that keeps bobbing up. A gang that we've trailed as far as Boston."

"Our summary," Doc Savage said, "leaves us where we started." The bronze man now issued instructions. "All of you get to the plane as soon as possible." He gave the location of the ship.

"Do not watch the plane so much as keep an eye open for persons who seem to have a suspicious interest in it," Doc said.

His explanation did not make much sense, and he did not elaborate upon it, but turned and walked away, and Monk and the others, after staring after him, puzzled, entered the limousine and drove off in the direction of the harbor where the plane was moored.

Doc Savage—this would have surprised Monk and the others—went back to Jason Lynn's hotel room and knocked on the door.

"What is it?" Jason Lynn called.

"Telegram marked urgent," Doc Savage said, changing his voice.

Jason Lynn opened the door. "I say! What . . . what—"

Doc walked in, closed the door, said quietly, "Sorry. I wanted to have another talk with you."

"I have no desire—"

"I was fairly certain you wouldn't have," Doc Savage said, and he took Jason Lynn by the neck with both hands and they began fighting.

Chapter XVII

TWO OF A KIND

At eleven o'clock that morning, tall, pompous Jason Lynn climbed from a cab in Charlestown, a part of Boston where the navy yard was located, and met a man who was waiting for him in front of a building near one of the gates to the naval base.

Jason Lynn was carrying something in a brief case, and he handled the bag carefully.

The man who met Jason Lynn was outstanding in neither appearance nor dress; quite plain and quiet-spoken, he appeared to be a foreigner of some sort.

Jason Lynn asked, "The meeting has been arranged?"

The man nodded. "The deal, if satisfactory, will be closed today."

They got in another cab, rode for some time as the quiet stranger gave directions to the driver. Somewhere north of Boston, near the water front, they got out and the man led Jason Lynn to an old house squatting like a fat hen near a row of docks.

"In here," the man directed.

101

The cab left. Apparently the neighborhood was deserted. The house was the only one in the vicinity, and even the windows were boarded. The two men went inside.

To Jason Lynn, the stranger said, "You understand, I believe, that you are to go blindfolded? That was the orders from our leader."

"Quite," said Jason Lynn.

He was quickly blindfolded, led down a flight of stairs and along a passageway. The tunnel apparently ended beneath a dock, because there was the salty smell of the ocean and the sound of foghorns offshore.

Jason Lynn was led up a gangplank, across a deck, down a companionway and into a darkened cabin. Soon there was the throb of engines, and the boat cast off.

For some time, Jason Lynn was left in the cabin. He was permitted to remove the blindfold, but he noted that the porthole opening had been painted black on the outside. Lights were turned on within the cabin. There was no way to tell whether the vessel was heading out to sea, or moving up the coast line.

Jason picked the lock rather expertly. Then he eased open the door and stepped out into a passageway; a moment later he was gliding along the corridor.

Voices were talking behind a closed cabin door farther along the gloomy passageway. For some moments, Jason Lynn listened. When there was movement inside the cabin, as if the occupants were preparing to leave, he hurried back to his own room.

He had not been able to understand the voices in the cabin.

About two hours later, throbbing of the boat's motors stopped and shortly the vessel bumped against something that might have been a wharf—or another boat. There was no motion except a gentle rocking.

The quiet, plain-looking man who had first met Jason Lynn returned to the cabin, said, "All right. Bring your case. The boss is here."

Jason Lynn was escorted to another cabin. In the room were seated several men who were obviously hired thugs. The one person who did not look like a gunman was masked and sat behind a large desk across the cabin.

In a quiet, well-modulated voice, he said, "You have the plans for your device with you?"

The Englishman, instead of answering the question directly, said, "I am ready to make a deal. The U. S. government is ready to pay a handsome price for my invention, sir. If your offer is sufficient, however, that is a different story."

"One thing," said the masked man seated opposite. "You are positive that your device can stop this—well, shall we give it the name the newspapers are beginning to use—the angry ghost?"

"Absolutely," said Jason Lynn. "It has been tested—though U. S. army officials think I am still working on it. They need that device, sir, to stop the havoc being wrought by—yes, we might as well call it the angry ghost."

The masked man smiled thinly. "Fine! We'll give you a million dollars for those plans. And I would like to close the deal here and now."

"You have the currency?"

The masked man placed a suitcase on the desk and opened it. It was full of bills of large denomination.

Jason Lynn stood up, opened his briefcase, dumped out a stack of perfectly blank papers.

Yelps of rage came from the hard-faced men seated in the cabin. The masked man demanded, "What kind of a trick is this?"

Very calmly, Jason Lynn said, "No trick, my dear man. I merely wanted to know that you meant what you said about buying my invention. The real plans are safe in a vault at my hotel. I shall be glad to return with them later, and you can have the money ready. Meanwhile, I must add a little to my price."

"Price? What do you mean?"

"Simply this," said Jason Lynn. "I happen to know that you are holding two people captive. One is my niece, Annabel Lynn. The other is her friend, Warren Allen. They must be put ashore with me and set free. Otherwise the deal is off!"

The masked man gave a start. Then he said, "You're quite a clever person, sir."

They used care—the long ride in the boat, then the blindfold was put on his eyes—in returning Jason Lynn to the shore somewhere north of Boston. It was dark when the boat put in, and apparently the trip had occupied the long period of time in order to make source of the contact confusing.

Jason Lynn got a surprise as soon as he stepped on shore.

Young Warren Allen and blond Annabel Lynn rushed to him, the girl crying, "Uncle Jason!" She was almost in tears as she kissed him.

"Great Scott!" gasped Jason Lynn. "How did you get here? I thought they had you prisoner?"

"They did. They just put us ashore!"

Jason Lynn saw now that the vessel that had brought him was a sleek, fast yacht. The quiet-looking man who had originally met him called down from the deck:

"We are returning your niece and her friend to you as a gesture to show you that we are straight shooters. We finish our deal tomorrow night. The place: Kittery Point near Portsmouth. You will find an old shack exactly one mile north of the Point, at a small inlet. Wait until you see a signal from offshore at ten o'clock."

Jason Lynn called, "Quite clear. I shall bring the plans with me. Have the money ready."

At the hotel entrance, Warren Allen said, "I have an errand to do, my dear. I take it you're going to Kittery Point too?"

The blond, tall girl nodded. "Call me later. We can catch a train first thing in the morning." She hooked her arm through her uncle's. "We'll all go together. And Warren—thanks for not asking questions. You're sweet for helping without knowing what it is all about."

Warren Allen departed, and the girl and Jason Lynn hurried to Jason's room.

Once inside, Annabel Lynn drew up short, gave a startled gasp, and stared from the Jason Lynn with her to the Jason Lynn waiting across the room.

There were, it appeared, two pompous Jason Lynns!

But the Jason Lynn with the girl—the one who had made the trip—placed his hands on his face, twisted at his features, and waxlike substance and the walrus mustaches came off. From his eyes, he removed small colored glass shells that had concealed orbs of rich flake-gold. From beneath his clothing, he removed padding that had made him look stout.

Annabel Lynn cried, "Why . . . you . . . you're Doc Savage!"

Doc said, "Quite!" His English accent was perfect.

Doc said to the girl's real uncle into whose arms she had now run, "The place is Kittery Point, near Portsmouth, tomorrow night."

The real Jason Lynn looked startled. "That's almost on top of Fort Smith!"

"Exactly," said Doc. "They plan to kill two birds with one stone. You had better proceed there by train. Do nothing that will arouse their suspicions." Doc explained about the signal that was to be given at ten o'clock, at the inlet near Kittery Point. "My men will be close by."

The bronze man looked at blond Annabel Lynn.

"I don't understand this," the girl said.

"Your uncle and I came to an agreement," Doc explained. "We fought a little, then we made up. We understand each other now—we have decided to work together."

Nodding to Jason Lynn, Doc went out. Half an hour later, at the harbor water front, a navy gig ferried him out to the large plane that was being guarded by his men.

Monk, Ham, Renny and Long Tom were there.

Nanny Hanks, who had been seated out of sight in the rear of the plane cabin, now came forward.

Monk pointed at Nanny Hanks.

"She cropped up again," he explained.

Nanny Hanks grinned. "I wanted to be in on the ghost-catching," she said.

Chapter XVIII

THE ANGRY GHOST ARRIVES

Later that night, Doc Savage's group, with equipment, moved northward from Boston Harbor in Doc's large plane. The bronze man himself was at the controls, and towering Renny, the engineer, did the navigating—and the navigating was no small task, because the night was very dark. On board were Long Tom, Monk, Ham and Nanny Hanks, and the cabin of the ship was crowded with a weird assortment of scientific apparatus and devices.

Doc said, "We'll land somewhere just north of the river entrance to Portsmouth, Maine."

Doc had a map in his hands and now he spread it out; he indicated various positions on the map. "Monk, you will go here with one of the sound-detector devices—one of the electrical listeners such as the army and navy uses to locate planes. We have several along."

Doc moved his finger a trifle on the map. "Long Tom will be *here*. And Ham, you cover *this* point. All of you will carry short-wave radio equipment and report any movement of anything out at sea, or in the air. I will be somewhere near *here*." The bronze man indicated another point, the isolated inlet near Kittery Point.

Doc returned to the controls; Renny had been flying. It was Doc who brought the huge plane down, near dawn, at a spot on a lonesome shore line below Kittery Point. The bronze man explained:

"We have about six hours start. But there is no time to lose."

They taxied the huge ship to shore and started unloading; afterward Doc directed the concealing of the big plane with branches and foliage cut on shore.

Monk got Doc Savage aside, asked, "Say, Doc, about this sour-puss, Nanny Hanks. I don't trust her. We know she's not a government agent. By havin' her around, ain't we harboring a viper in our bosoms, as the sayin' goes?"

Doc said, "Nanny Hanks is a very clever operative of the United States government," he stated. "She pretended to be a fake in order to get in with foreign secret agents and learn their movements. What she has accomplished has never been done by any other woman operative."

The day was quiet—a cocked-gun kind of quiet. Concealed at vital points along the rocky coast line, Doc's assistants used sound-detector devices. It was Ham who noted that all the detectors were placed in the vicinity of Fort Smith, adjacent to Kittery Point. Instructions to each man was to report immediately on any movement of anything out at sea, or in the air.

Doc had his other equipment installed in a shack at the isolated inlet at Kittery Point. Strangely, this seemed to include most of the bronze man's more antiquated apparatus.

Monk saw that Doc had simply gathered together a litter of apparatus that *looked* impressive.

Annabel Lynn, accompanied by her uncle, Jason, and Warren Allen arrived at nine that night. It was only an hour now to the appointed time when the contact was to be made.

The bronze man explained to Jason Lynn, his niece Annabel and Warren Allen, "You will stay ashore when the contact is made." Jason Lynn swallowed. "But—"

"Allow us to handle everything."

Shortly thereafter, Doc Savage put on the make-up that transformed him into a second pompous Jason Lynn. Lights were turned off inside the shack; they waited in silence. Fog rolled in from the Atlantic and clung wetly to clothing; there was the sound of surf on the nearby rocky shore, and frequent dismal croaking of night things in the darkness.

It was near ten when the radio began speaking in the darkness of the old shack. It was Long Tom's voice, and the electrical expert sounded excited.

"*Doc!*" Long Tom's voice came, "*Something out here offshore. It's heading for the inlet. Can't tell what the thing is, but there's powerful motor sound. Something that sounds like Diesels!*"

Speaking into the radio microphone, Doc advised, "*Return here at once.*"

In the following minutes, Renny, Monk and Ham each reported similar movement of the unseen vessel.

"Come back here at once," Doc directed each of them.

They assembled in a compact group—Jason Lynn, Annabel, Warren Allen, Monk, Ham, Renny, Long Tom, Nanny Hanks and Doc Savage.

Doc Savage said, "We will separate now, and meet at the shack down by the beach. We can go more quietly one at a time. I will go first. The rest of you scatter, and make your way as silently as you can to the shack.

The bronze man left the others, moved rapidly, and was soon lost to sight in the night.

When Monk and Ham reached the shack, they discovered Renny and Long Tom already there. Some time later, Warren Allen put in an appearance, then Nanny Hanks.

There was quite a delay before Annabel Lynn and her uncle, Jason Lynn, arrived. And not long thereafter, Doc Savage joined them.

The bronze man indicated the shack in which he had placed the conglomeration of apparatus.

"As you know," he said, "Jason Lynn had invented a method of ending this fantastic menace that has become known as the angry ghost.

"Unknown to any of you, we visited the laboratory," Doc continued, "and secured the necessary apparatus, which we have assembled here in this shack. We are about to test the effectiveness of our machinery."

"You think the angry ghost is going to pop up around here?" Monk asked innocently.

"Exactly," Doc said.

"And the gadget in there"—Monk pointed at the shack—"will lay the ghost. That the idea?"

"Yes."

Monk couldn't help snorting. "What makes you so sure the angry ghost, as they call it, is going to be here?"

"The submarine is approaching," Doc said.

"Sub— Holy cow!" Renny rumbled. "That *was* what I picked up over the listener."

Doc said, "The submarine probably brought the angry ghost to those forts where the gun bases were damaged, and it must have been lying in the East River when the bridge collapsed in New York City."

"But what about the Treasury Building collapse in Washington, the attack on our headquarters when your instruments were smashed, and some other times."

"Recall the truck in which you were hauled about in Washington, when you were prisoners?" Doc asked. "Half of the truck body was partitioned off, I believe you said."

"Yes." Monk's jaw fell. "Great Scott, Doc! You mean we were riding around with the *thing* in the other half of that truck?"

"Very likely. And you recall the sound truck which was following you toward New London—the sound truck we failed to capture? That truck was undoubtedly used to transport this—well, the angry ghost.

"For a time," Doc conceded, "I was on the wrong trail. I thought the menace was coming from the air. I borrowed an army stratosphere plane, but did not find anything."

They could hear the submarine engines now without any aid from the supersensitive electrical pickups. The craft had moved into the cove, and seemed to be anchoring.

Doc said, "No time for more talk. Nanny Hanks—Jason Lynn—Annabel—Warren Allen—you four get up the hill to the right of this shack. Wait there. If anything happens to us—if we should fail to whip this thing—you will flee for your lives. Run for it. Get to the army or navy authorities and tell them all you know."

Jason Lynn, Annabel, Warren Allen and Nanny Hanks

left Doc Savage and the others. It was very dark. Jason Lynn led the way for the first few minutes; then Warren Allen spoke up in a hoarse whisper.

"Mr. Lynn," said Warren Allen, "aren't you losing your way? You're not heading for the hillock where Doc Savage told us to wait."

"Maybe I am getting lost in the dark," Jason Lynn said, rather gruffly.

Within the next few yards, Jason Lynn chose a convenient spot to stumble—a spot where there were plenty of rocks. When he stood up again, he carried a round rock, slightly larger than a baseball, in his fist.

Jason Lynn used the rock to strike Warren Allen on the head. Warren Allen dropped, instantly senseless.

"You want me to tie him?" Nanny Hanks asked calmly.

"Yes," said Jason Lynn. "Tie him and gag him. We've got a lot to do, and not many minutes to do it."

Chapter XIX

THE GHOST LAYING

Doc Savage gathered his men on the beach and said, "Now here is the plan. I am going out as Jason Lynn, presumably carrying the designs for the device to stop the angry ghost. After I reach the submarine, you raid the submarine. Close in fast, and if we make a good surprise attack, we may be able to whip them."

"How do we get out to the sub?" Ham asked.

"Better swim," Doc said. "They would spot a boat." The bronze man moved into some nearby bushes and came out with several small sacks filled with ordinary cork fishnet floats such as fishermen use.

"Here are floats," he said. "After you get in the water, discard corks until these will just keep you on the surface. If searchlights are swung toward you, you must be able to submerge and stay under until the light moves on."

"But Doc," Monk gulped. "What if this angry ghost takes a hand in the fight?"

Doc was already moving down to the beach. He did not answer.

A boat came from the submarine.

"Jason Lynn," called a quiet voice.

"Here," Doc said. He looked and sounded like Jason Lynn.

"Get in the boat," he was ordered.

Moments later he was in the small rowboat and pulling out of the inlet. A searchlight sprang toward them from close offshore, and Doc knew that there was deep water all around here. It was easy for the sub—he knew that it was the small submarine he had seen near New London—to come in close. The sub soon loomed out of the half-mist.

Looking back, Doc observed that objects on shore were indistinct seen from here. The men rowing the collapsible steel boat, two of them, said nothing.

The boat bumped the steel, dark sides of the submarine. Immediately, someone spoke. "Jason Lynn?"

"Yes," said Doc.

"Over this way," said the voice.

Then Doc Savage saw the speaker's figure, standing near a curved ladder that led overside. The bronze man swung aboard. He was immediately escorted down the hatch to the control room just below.

The quiet-looking man with the accent, the one who had contacted Doc the day before, stood in the small room that was lined with switchboards and devices for control of the submarine. Other men crowded in through a heavy steel bulkhead doorway. All were big and grim-faced and quiet.

There was no sign of the masked man.

The quiet-voiced man said, "I'm afraid this is as long as you fool us. *You see, we happen to know that you are Doc Savage.*"

Guns appeared, a ring of them that menaced the bronze man.

The fellow with the quiet voice was obviously elated. "We aren't fools, as you're discovering," he said. "We know that you talked to Jason Lynn, and persuaded him not to sell out to us, as well as help trap us."

One of the ring of men cocked his revolver and asked, "Now?"

"Not yet," the quiet-voiced man said quickly. "We

will let him live for a minute or two. He is a very famous man. He deserves a few moments and a few last words."

Doc said, "Good idea. You may not be as smooth as you thought."

"Eh?" They stared at him startled.

"When I went to the rear admiral in Washington and offered to help, I began to get an inkling of the truth," Doc Savage explained without particular emotion. "The navy didn't want the truth to get out—didn't want the world to know that an enemy could wander up and down our coast line with impunity, putting bridges and forts and guns out of commission. So my offer of help was refused—because things I do sometimes get into the newspapers."

The quiet man smiled. "You know, then, that my country is trying to borrow money from your United States?"

"Yes. I know, too, that your country was one of those which borrowed heavily from America during the World War, then repudiated its debt—as a result of which repudiation, America would refuse to make your nation a loan now."

"That is true. Why deny it?"

"So your country began a campaign of extortion. You started demolishing forts and bridges and public buildings. The idea was merely to create so much fantastic damage that you would force the United States to make the loan. In other words, you thought you would convince the government it was cheaper to make the loan than to suffer all this damage and embarrassing publicity."

"All quite true. What else do you know?"

"A secret agent of the United States government was serving as go-between for you and the United States government," Doc said. "The agent was a woman—Nanny Hanks."

The other smiled, but nodded. "Nanny Hanks must have told you that. So she is *really* a Federal agent! We thought she was a fake. Her credentials were forgeries."

"Deliberately forged to deceive you and others."

"Who would Nanny Hanks want to deceive beside ourselves?" The man was becoming intensely interested.

"Annabel Lynn, for one," Doc said.

"You know who Miss Lynn really is?"

"A secret agent for the English government," Doc said. "She was assigned to the task of finding the secret of—shall we continue to call it the angry ghost?"

"And her uncle, Jason Lynn?"

"An inventor, on the staff of the English army research department, who had perfected what he is convinced is a defense against the—angry ghost."

The quiet man smiled thinly. "That term—the angry ghost—is childish," he said. "Suppose we call the device by its true designation."

"Which is?"

"A sonic cohesion destroyer," the man explained. "By the way, we also happen to know that Jason Lynn furnished this apparatus, a neutralizing device, and that you have it set up in a shack on shore, on the chance you might get an opportunity to use it. I think we will destroy that shack and the apparatus now, then send a raiding party ashore to find the real Jason Lynn."

The "sonic cohesion destroyer," as the man had termed it, was mounted on an elevator so that it could be lifted out through a hatch in the submarine deck. The contrivance was in place, a highly complicated assortment of electrical mechanism—tubes, wires, coils—and big parabolic reflectors.

"Did you," said the quiet-voiced man, "ever see an opera singer break a wineglass by singing close to it?"

"It is a well-known trick," Doc admitted.

"That explains, in a general way, how our device functions," the man advised. "Every object has a vibrating point, and that is why the wineglass, for instance, breaks. We have gone a step farther—or our inventors did—and discovered that every molecule of matter has a vibrating point. In other words, when subjected to a certain wavelength of combination sonic and electric nature, any molecule can be so disturbed—not shattered, mind you, but disturbed—that it loses its cohesion with other molecules."

"And cohesion is destroyed? The object falls to dust?"

"Exactly."

"You explain it very simply," Doc said. "You must be familiar with it."

"I am Ambrose Zoanisti," said the man proudly. "I helped perfect the device."

"I see." Doc made his voice properly impressed. "And you are going to destroy Jason Lynn's apparatus for breaking up your sonic-electrical wave with a counter wave of similar nature. The apparatus which you say you know is in that shack?"

"I am."

Ambrose began manipulating controls of the apparatus. It was quite a complicated process, and twice he swore violently before he got the readings of meters balanced to suit him.

"Searchlights!" he barked sharply.

Searchlight beams from the submarine lunged toward shore, impaled the old shack, and held it.

Ambrose jerked a switch. There was some hissing and buzzing from the apparatus, and Doc Savage was conscious of a terrific trembling, uncontrollable and utterly unpleasant, which seized his body. Striving to control his muscles, he looked around, and saw that the trembling had seized the others, as well.

Ambrose saw that Doc Savage was alarmed, and gave a wolfish, trembling smile.

"Merely a vibratory harmonic setup in the vicinity of the cohesion-destroying beam," Ambrose said. "Very unpleasant, but not harmful—unless your body is subjected to it for too long a period."

Doc watched the shack. It slowly crumbled and fell, turning into a cloud of smoky-looking dust, which settled after squirming around in the glare of the searchlights.

"You see," said Ambrose proudly.

Doc Savage had glanced about—and seen Monk. The homely chemist was close to the hull of the submarine. A few moments more of diversion were needed to enable Monk and the others to get aboard; Doc furnished it with a remark.

"The shack," he said, "merely held some old apparatus from my laboratory—stuff that looked impressive enough to fool the man we wanted to fool."

"Fool the man—" Ambrose gave a violent start, ogled Doc Savage.

Doc nodded. "You see," he said, "we knew another thing

—we knew the identity of your boss. We knew who was really in charge of this trouble."

Before the other could make any comment on that, Monk and the others came up over the side of the submarine. There was a guttural shout, and instant confusion.

Doc Savage had been searched, but not bound. He wrenched off his coat, threw it down, stamped on it— making sure his shoe soles crunched certain buttons on the coat, and these broke into sizzling flame and the whole coat began smoldering and giving off evil-looking vapor which came from the chemicals with which the coat was saturated.

Doc threw the coat down the hatch. Gas from the blazing garment would uncontrollably sicken anyone unlucky enough to get into the stuff.

Doc himself managed to tie his handkerchief over his mouth. The handkerchief, a thick fibrous cloth saturated with chemicals, was a filter which would serve as a fairly effective gas mask.

Monk and others were wearing similar handkerchief masks.

Doc lunged at Ambrose as the man leaped away from the intricate sonic cohesion destroyer apparatus. He swung a fist. Ambrose made a barking sound, walked backward; his knees hit the rail and he flipped over into the sea.

Renny was howling, swinging his big fists. Whenever he missed a blow, he all but followed his huge fist into the air. When he did not miss, he bruised flesh or broke bones.

Monk had started his usual howling. He had two men down, was trying to roll with them into the sea.

Ham had bad luck, and lost his sword-cane before he got a chance to use it. A man snatched the weapon, hurled it into the sea.

Long Tom, standing clear of the general mêlée, unlimbered one of the supermachine pistols—small weapons, not much larger than automatics—which spouted mercy bullets, slugs which produced quick unconsciousness without doing much physical damage.

There were not many men on deck. The fight was fairly even. They stood a good chance of winning—until someone in the sub control room began filling the ballast tanks and submerging the underseas craft.

The sub went down quickly, with crash-dive speed. Men were fighting to get the hatches closed.

Monk fought clear of his opponents, raced along the deck, and grabbed the painter of the collapsible boat. But instead of leaping into the boat, he yanked the little craft up bodily on deck.

The collapsible boat was not heavy, and Monk was fabulously strong. Monk jammed the small craft, bow-first, into the handiest deck hatch opening. He remained there, fighting off men who tried to get the boat out of the hatch, until water came boiling up over the deck and washed him away.

Monk had effectively prevented the closing of the hatch, so that a flood of sea water poured into the craft as it sank.

Doc, diving clear of the swirl of water, lifted his voice.

"Flares!" he shouted. "Use flares."

The flares were small pellets, magnesium combined with other chemicals, which floated and burned with intense glare, unhampered by water.

By that light, Doc Savage located Ambrose and another man swimming in the bay. He overhauled them, laid his fist against their jaws to produce unconsciousness, and towed them ashore.

The navy planes arrived shortly after midnight. They had been summoned by Doc Savage, using his portable radio, and they brought divers and diving equipment—as well as Real Admiral Benton.

Rear Admiral Benton was the high navy officer who had refused Doc Savage's help in Washington, and he was a little sheepish about the whole thing.

"We made an error in judgment," he said. "Although, as a matter of fact, we had been specifically warned that you were not to be called in to aid in the case."

"I understand," Doc said pleasantly.

"I fear the public won't," the rear admiral muttered. "Here is a little half-baked European country which was trying to extort a big loan from the United States, and going up and down our coast destroying military equipment and public structures at will. And we refused help from the one man who finally managed to corner the trouble-makers and overcome them—meaning yourself."

"The public need not know about this," Doc Savage said.

Rear Admiral Benton swallowed twice. "You mean that?" he asked.

"Of course." Newspaper publicity was one of the things which Doc Savage had found it wise to avoid whenever possible. He explained this. "Let it be known simply that the Federal government cornered the extortionists and overcame them. As a matter of fact, that is what happened. As you know, I have a Federal commission as a secret agent, as well as a commission as a naval officer, retired."

The divers came in and reported.

"There are a number of the gang alive in the sub," they explained. "They can be gotten out alive. The water where the craft is lying is not deep."

"How about the apparatus they were using—the sonic cohesion destroyer?"

"It can be lifted intact."

"Get it up," the rear admiral ordered grimly. "We'll put that thing in the vaults at headquarters, along with some other little surprise weapons we're saving for anybody foolish enough to force this country into a war."

The matter as a whole had been satisfactorily settled. Of the extortionists—they were no better than extortionists, although they had been attempting to work on an international plane—had been caught, those who had not drowned when the submarine sank.

Monk cornered Doc. "Enlighten me on some things. Nanny Hanks misled you in the first place. She sent you on a wild-goose chase to that reservoir in Washington, remember? She said we were being held prisoner there."

"At that time," Doc explained, "Nanny Hanks had orders to keep us from becoming involved in the mystery. The government, you understand, was in a predicament. It hoped to solve the thing without our help. Specific orders had come from the foreign extortionists to keep us out of it, and that was what Nanny Hanks was trying to do."

"What about when she sent you to that reservoir? Nanny Hanks said we were there, and we weren't even prisoners. Instead, you almost fell into a trap."

"Nanny Hanks was trying to help me get on the trail of the gang. She didn't approve of her orders to keep me out of it. She knew the gang had been using that reservoir hide-out. The government, you know, had learned a great deal about this gang."

"Nanny Hanks knew the bridge was going to collapse. How come?"

"The extortionists, for the greater effect, had notified the government that bridge would fall at a certain time. The bridge was heavily guarded—but not against a submarine and a fantastic shattering device such as this gadget."

Monk nodded, said, "But two or three other things bumfoozle me. Who sent that note to entice Annabel out to the Staten Island fort—looking for her uncle?"

"The extortionists wrote it. They were trying to get their hands on the girl."

"Her uncle wasn't even there?"

"Of course not," Doc said. "He was in Boston. If she had taken the time to check with that Boston hotel where he lived, she would have found him safe. I merely checked with the hotel later, and found him without difficulty. I got her uncle's address, incidentally, from officials of the intelligence department in Washington, who knew it."

Monk pondered. "Why were the instruments shattered in your lab, Doc?"

"To bumfoozle us, as you put it. The gang evidently had two of these gadgets, and they used one on my office at exactly the time they worked on the Treasury Building in Washington. That was to confuse us—two menaces striking in different places at the same time, and that sort of thing."

"It was pretty involved," Monk said gloomily. "Guess we never will understand why they did some of the things they did."

The one point unsettled was the disposition of Annabel Lynn and her Uncle Jason.

"Technically, they are foreign secret agents, and therefore liable to arrest and prosecution," said Rear Admiral Benton. "However"—he studied Doc Savage thoughtfully —"I think we shall ask you for suggestions about that."

Doc's reply was prompt. The Lynns were instrumental in capturing the real head of the plot in America," he pointed out. "This way, and we'll show you."

The bronze man guided them to a spot in the brush nearby, where a bound figure lay. The bound man glared at them, said several things, using words which could not be found in any dictionary.

"Warren Allen!" Monk exploded.

"The leader of that submarine gang," Doc said. "Warren Allen signaled them with a flashlight as they were coming into the cove tonight. That is how they happened to know about the fake apparatus we rigged in the shack. As a matter of fact, that is why we did so much futile chasing about throughout the affair. Warren Allen was keeping them posted as to our moves."

Warren Allen was handcuffed and hauled away.

Monk watched him go with considerable pleasure.

"That," said Monk, "leaves the coast clear for me, as far as Annabel Lynn is concerned."

DOC SAVAGE

To the world at large, Doc Savage is a strange, mysterious figure of glistening bronze skin and golden eyes. To his fans he is the greatest adventure hero of all time, whose fantastic exploits are unequaled for hair-raising thrills, breathtaking escapes, blood-curdling excitement!

☐	THE EVIL GNOME	2134	$1.25
☐	THE MAN OF BRONZE	6352	$1.25
☐	THE STONE MAN	6419	$1.25
☐	THE BOSS OF TERROR	6424	$1.25
☐	THE THOUSAND HEADED MAN	6471	$1.25
☐	THE RED TERRORS	6486	$1.25
☐	DOC SAVAGE: HIS APOCALYPTIC LIFE	8834	$1.25
☐	THE KING MAKER	10042	$1.25
☐	THE PHANTOM CITY	10119	$1.25
☐	THE MYSTIC MULLAH	10120	$1.25
☐	FEAR CAY	10121	$1.25
☐	LAND OF ALWAYS NIGHT	10122	$1.25
☐	FANTASTIC ISLAND	10125	$1.25
☐	QUEST OF QUI	10126	$1.25

Buy them at your local bookstore or use this handy coupon for ordering:

THE EXCITING REALM OF STAR TREK

☐ STAR TREK LIVES!
  by Lichtenberg, Marshak & Winston
                                  2151 • $1.95
☐ STAR TREK: The NEW VOYAGES
  by Culbreath & Marshak   2719 • $1.75

THRILLING ADVENTURES IN INTERGALACTIC SPACE
BY JAMES BLISH

☐ SPOCK MUST DIE!   2245   • $1.25
☐ STAR TREK 1   2114   • $1.25
☐ STAR TREK 2   2171   • $1.25
☐ STAR TREK 3   2253   • $1.25
☐ STAR TREK 4   2172   • $1.25
☐ STAR TREK 5   8150   • $1.25
☐ STAR TREK 6   8154   • $1.25
☐ STAR TREK 7   2240   • $1.25
☐ STAR TREK 8   2250   • $1.25
☐ STAR TREK 9   2238   • $1.25
☐ STAR TREK 10   10796 • $1.50
☐ STAR TREK 11   8717   • $1.25

Buy them at your local bookstore or use this handy coupon for ordering: